AF272956

Don't Lie to Me Young Lady

Sue Armstrong

novum pro

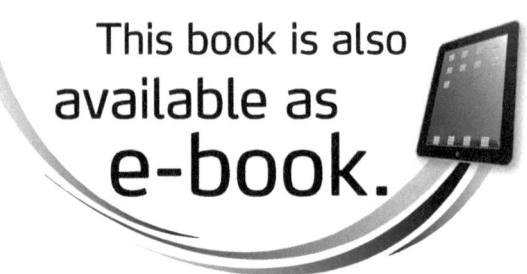

www.novum-publishing.co.uk

© 2023 novum publishing

ISBN 978-3-99131-905-4
Editing: Hugo Chandler, BA
Cover photo:
Dragoscondrea | Dreamstime.com
Cover design, layout & typesetting:
novum publishing

www.novum-publishing.co.uk

Climate neutral
Print product
ClimatePartner.com/16547-2201-1002

Chapter One

Mia

On the outskirts of a small town, there was a large home painted white. The people who lived there, Lord and Lady Swan, were very wealthy. They had servants who loved the family and liked working for them.

The nanny was in charge of three children; two girls and a boy. Nanny did not have any children of her own nor was she married; so living with the family was the best job she could think of. Then, there was the gardener who was good at looking after the rose bushes and making sure the lawns were kept in good order. He was married and had two sons who were just about to leave school and start working as gardeners.

The cook was a large lady who had rosy cheeks. She made delicious meals for everyone, so even the staff looked forward to her dinners.

One January morning, when the ground was hard with frost, a baby girl was born to the mistress of the house. The doctor came downstairs to announce to the staff. "My Lady has given birth to a lovely girl and both mother and baby are doing well." He asked the cook to take a cup of tea and a light meal up to the room and said that she had to rest.

Later that morning, the nanny took the three children to their mother's room to see the new arrival. Nanny said. "She is gorgeous, My Lady; have you got a name for her?"

"Yes she will be known as Mia."

The three children started to dance around the room chanting.

The nanny said. "Come on children let's leave Mia to get some sleep."

Going downstairs, Linda, the eldest girl, said she would make a card for her mother and her sister Mia, while Graham and Paulette went outside to play.

Kevin and Sonya, the parents, were so smitten with Mia that they named a rose after her. Mr Hebden found a rose in his catalogue that would be perfect. It was white with a pink tip at its fringe. So, after showing it to his master, he ordered a bush. It took almost one week before it was delivered. Kevin said he knew just where he wanted the roses to be planted in the garden, right under the nursery window.

Miss Thomas the nanny was sitting at the table talking to Mrs Richardson the cook about Mia and planning the christening, the food that would be needed and the baby gown Mia would be wearing for her big day. The family would, as required by tradition, normally make it an elaborate event that lasted all day.

"It will happen in two weeks," said Miss Thomas. "Plenty of time to make a cake."

Mr Parr the chauffeur had to make sure the car was cleaned and ready for the big day. He wanted to put fresh flowers on the back shelf of the car, so he spoke to Mr Hebden to see what flowers would be ready that morning. After choosing them, Mr. Hebden put a pink ribbon around the plants so that he could pick them fresh on the morning of the christening.

The vicar came to the house to talk to Kevin and Sonya. They decided on the date and time and started to send out invitations. Linda, Graham and Paulette had new clothes to wear. Kevin wore a morning suit with red lining on the inside of the jacket, Sonya had a long duck blue dress with short sleeves. On the morning of the christening when they were all in their finery, they posed for a family photograph, but then Kevin stopped the photo shoot as he had forgotten something. Running upstairs, he went into his office and opened one of his desk drawers and came down holding a long box, giving it to Sonya.

"To my darling, for giving me another daughter," he said. "Mia is perfect."

Sonya opened the box and took out a pearl necklace. Kevin fastened it around her neck and they had another photo taken for the album.

The party went on until the early hours as most of their parties did and Mia was an angel all day.

The family was happy until Kevin had to go on a trip, which would take him away from home for about three months. So, packing his suitcase, he took a photo of the family to put next to his bed. He had never left his family before, but he had to go on the trip to see his mother, whom he had been told was very ill. They had not seen each other for years as she did not like the way he had spent the family fortune. All his wealth came from his father's family, but his dad ensured that his mother was taken care of. She had servants and a lovely house to live in, but she was lonely. Friends are only friends but the family is the real thing and sometimes they are so far away it's hard for them to visit.

Kevin went out one day to see his mother's solicitor to ask if he could let him know if his mother had money problems. "I know my father had provided for her, but he died many years ago and money can soon run out." The lawyer told Kevin he was sure his mother was still wealthy and if he did find she was short of money, he would let Kevin know.

On his way back to his mother's home, Kevin met a woman who was much younger than he was and she started to flirt with him. Kevin thought he could take her out for a meal and get to know her better, but he was a married man and his mother was not well. He asked her for her phone number and said he would call and arrange for them to go out for a drink or a meal. That was the beginning that would break his family apart.

Kevin started to see Shirley on most days. They would walk along the country lanes, go for meals at the local restaurant and have a drink after she finished work. She worked at the local ball bearing factory as a cleaner although she thought she was worth more than that. When Kevin told her he was married with four children, the youngest being a few weeks old, that did not put her off. Once she had determined how rich he was, she had to get her claws into him. She started to plan how she could get some money and she told Kevin that she needed to find her rent money or she would be evicted. Kevin was a soft touch when it came to women.

Kevin's mother was starting to feel better. She would sit outside in the garden wrapped up in a warm blanket, reading her book and drinking a hot cup of tea. When Kevin came to visit, she looked up at him.

"I love sitting out in this beautiful garden," she said, "the birds are singing." They sang all the time, but it made it more special now that Kevin was with her.

Sonya phoned Kevin to ask when he thought he would be home. "She is feeling much better now so I should be home soon. How are the children, is Mia growing?"

"Yes," said Sonya. "She misses you as all of us do."

"Tell the children I will be home soon and give them my love, bye love," Kevin said, hanging up.

Kevin packed his case and said goodbye to his mother. "I will visit soon, but in the meantime, if you need anything, let me know."

"I will son, thank you for coming to see me."

With that, Kevin left the house and entered a taxi heading for the station.

Looking out of the window, he saw Shirley walking along the street all dolled up. Kevin thought she was at work, but it must have been her day off. Telling the taxi driver to stop, he rolled down the window.

"Hello there," Kevin said. "Are you going somewhere nice?"

Shirley turned her head to see Kevin sitting in the taxi. "Oh hello. I am just going to see a friend. It's girls' day out."

Kevin asked if she would like a lift. "That's kind of you to ask," she said.

Shirley climbed into the taxi.

As they chatted, Kevin said. "Did you manage to get your rent money sorted?"

"No. I must see if my friend can help me."

Kevin put his hand inside his pocket, to get some money to give to Shirley. She put it into her handbag and told the taxi driver to stop. She got out of the taxi, and without looking back, started to walk in the opposite direction. Kevin made his way back home thinking he had been made a fool of.

Arriving home, he could hear the children playing in the garden. It was a warm day. He saw Sonya sitting under a large parasol with Mia next to her in her pram.

"Daddy!" The children shouted and started to run towards him. He opened his arms wide to give them all a big hug.

Paulette asked. "Are you home for good now? We have missed you."

"Is grandmother feeling better?" Linda asked. Mia was fast asleep in her pram wrapped up in a shawl.

Sonya said, "She is so beautiful with her hair sticking up on the top of her head. She has been excellent and she has gained a little weight."

Kevin picked Mia up to hug her. She stretched as he kissed her. "Hello, my little angel. Daddy is home."

After the evening meal, Kevin and Sonya sat in the lounge by the fire, talking about his mother. "She is doing very well. I spoke to her solicitor to see how her finances were doing. He tells me she is still wealthy, but if anything changes, he will let me know."

"That's good to know," said Sonya. "We must go and visit her in the summer and take the children. I am sure she would love to see them."

The children's tutor Miss Evens was due back the following week. She bought some books for the children to read before the term started. This was good news for the girls but Graham wanted to play soccer.

"No," said Kevin. "You must read one of the books Miss Evens bought for you."

Looking through them, Graham picked one and took it to his room. Lying on his bed, he started to read. He had read almost half of the book when there was a knock on his door. It was his mother who said it was time to put the book down and get into bed.

Kissing the top of his head, Sonya said, "Good night my darling."

"Good night, Mummy," said Graham. Snuggling down under the covers Graham fell fast asleep.

The next morning Graham was up early. He dressed and headed downstairs with a book in his hand. Cook had made breakfast, and it was ready in the dining room. Sitting at the table was his father reading the newspaper.

"Good morning, Daddy," said Graham.

Putting the newspaper down, Kevin replied. "Good morning son. How are you today?

"Well thank you." Graham put the book down on the table and went to the sideboard to help himself to bacon and eggs.

Kevin saw the book and read the title it was called 'Up in the Sky'.

"Is it a good book," Kevin asked.

"Yes," said Graham with the biggest smile on his face, and with that, the girls arrived for breakfast, each holding a book.

Linda's book was titled 'On the Front Line' and Paulette's book was titled, 'Little Nurse'.

Miss Evens arrived early to start her lessons. The children were so excited to tell their tutor what the stories were about. She was pleased to hear that they could not put the books down and that they were planning what books they wanted to read after they had finished these. After, the lessons were over the children spent the evening with their parents.

Kevin started to wonder what was happening to Shirley and so after a few days, he plucked up the courage to give her a ring. She started to cry and said she had to move out of her lodgings as the owner had some new tenants moving in. She had tried finding another place but to no avail, and with that, Kevin said he would find a place and that he would let her know the progress as soon as possible.

He phoned a friend who ran a hotel to ask if he had a spare room for a few weeks. He then phoned Shirley to tell her that she had a room close to her work so she would not need to catch a bus every day.

Telling her landlord, she was moving out on the weekend she started to pack her possessions into boxes and got one of her workmates to help with moving her belongings into her room at the hotel. Shirley thought she was moving up the ladder.

After a couple of months, Kevin told Sonya that he wanted to see his mother for a few days. He booked his train ticket, packed his case and set off for the train.

Arriving at his mother's house, Kevin spent some time with her talking about the children. He asked how things were with her and if her health was improving. She said that she had a doctor visit the week before as she had a chest infection. He put her on antibiotics and it was almost cleared-up. She asked Kevin how long he was staying, and he told her he had some business in town, so he would be there for a few days.

Kevin arranged to meet Shirley that evening. They went out for a drink and then back to her room in the hotel. They talk for hours. Shirley asked if he was staying the night. Kevin said he was staying at his mother's but would stay a little longer. They lay down on the bed kissing. One thing led to another and running her hands down his back, Shirley stopped at his bum. They looked at each other and after more kissing, they had sex again.

Kevin rolled over onto his back and said, "That was fantastic." He had a big smile on his face. After an hour, he got dressed and headed back to his mother's home.

The next day, after Shirley had finished work they went out for a meal. While they were holding hands, the people at the next table looked as though they knew Kevin. After some whispering, the man said, "It is you. I thought it was you Kevin. You and your wife came to our dinner party a couple of years ago."

Trying to think who these people were, Kevin suddenly remembered they were the Wilsons. Mr. Wilson was the bank manager of the local bank who had retired the year before.

"Hello, how are you doing?" Kevin asked. "Are you enjoying retirement?"

"Yes," replied Mrs Wilson. "We can do more now that he doesn't have to go into the office."

Looking at Shirley, Mr Wilson asked. "And who is this?"

"Oh this is my friend Shirley," said Kevin, and with that Shirley wanted to leave.

Kevin asked the waiter for the bill, paid and said goodnight to the Wilsons.

Heading back to the hotel, Shirley asked Kevin if she could have a word with him. That was an excuse to make love again. She loved having sex, the more she could get it the better she felt.

This went on for a couple of years and Sonya had no idea that Kevin was having an affair. When he could not cover up his feelings for Shirley any longer, he told Sonya he was leaving her to set up home with Shirley and that she was pregnant. Sonya was devastated. They had the biggest argument ever and Kevin told her that it had started when he had gone visiting his mother when she was ill and he had met Shirley then. Kevin told the children and his staff that he was leaving but that things would continue as normal. The children were upset about this news, although Mia didn't understand as she was too young.

Years later, the news arrived that Shirley had had another child and that Kevin was missing his other children so much that he wanted them to go and stay with him and Shirley. Sonya was unhappy about this and got in touch with her solicitor, who said that it would benefit the children to spend time with their father. After thinking about it, Sonya asked the children if they wanted to go and stay with their father for a short while.

"Why?" Said Linda. "Do you not want us anymore?"

"I will always want you darling, but your father is missing you and he wants you all to go and stay with him." The children looked at each other and then back at their mother, who had tears in her eyes. Linda said that they would go for a short while and then come back home to her. Sonya told Kevin he could come and collect the children, but he could only have them for two weeks, then they had to be returned to her.

Kevin arrived the next day to collect his children and then took them on the train to meet Shirley.

At first, Shirley seemed to like the children, but when Kevin had to go and meet some acquaintances and, she had to look after six children she did not like it. The older children could entertain themselves, but Mia was too young to read a book and needed attention. So, when the older children were out in the garden, Shirley would hit Mia even though she had not done anything wrong. After two weeks the children went back to their mother.

Arriving back home, Sonya hugged them. Cook had made them lunch and nanny was so pleased to see them that she even gave each of them a kiss. That evening, when the nanny had put the children to bed after they had their bath, she went downstairs to have a word with Sonya.

"My Lady can I have a word with you about the children? Mia to be precise."

Sonya told the nanny to take a seat and asked her what the matter was. Nanny took a deep breath and said that when she was bathing Mia, she found marks on her back.

"It looked like she had been whipped," Nanny said.

"What!" Said Sonya. "Whipped! Who could do a thing like that."

Sonya went upstairs to look at Mia's back and sure enough, there were marks on her baby's back. Shaking, Sonya had to sit down and Nanny went to get her a stiff drink. When Nanny went back upstairs, Sonya had her head in her hands, crying.

"My Lady here have this," Nanny said, handing a glass of whisky.

Sonya took a sip and placed the glass on a table. "I must phone the police straight away and report this." Thinking she should tell Kevin, Sonya decided to wait until the police had been to see her.

Cook answered the door and showed the police officers to the lounge where Sonya was waiting with the nanny.

"Hello," said Sonya, "please take a seat."

The officers sat down and took out their notebooks. They started to write down what Sonya had told them. They wanted to know where her husband was living and whom she thought had done this to her child.

The only person Sonya could think of was Shirley, but she could not say for sure, and as for where her husband lived, she would have to phone him to get his address. The officers had enough details to work with and a officer asked if they could take photos of Mia's back. The nanny took him upstairs to Mia's room. Nanny lifted Mia's nightdress so that the officer could take the photo. He took a big gulp of air and said, "Poor thing." After taking quite a few photos he left the room and thanked the nanny. He spoke to Sonya and said they would be in touch and then they left.

Sonya phoned Kevin to say that the children had loved being with him and asked if he would give her his address as the children wanted to send a picture to him.

"Yes, my address is 21, Northeast Gate, Forth Town."

Sonya phoned the police officers and gave them his address.

"Thank you we will pay him and this woman Shirley a visit. We will let you know how things go."

Sonya put the phone down and asked the cook to make a special dinner for tonight. The children needed some time away from Shirley, so if their father wanted to see them, he would have to come to his wife's home.

The officers arrived at Kevin's home and asked to speak to him in private. At first, Kevin thought it was about his mother.

"No, sir, it's about one of your children, Mia."

"Mia," said Kevin. "What has happened is she okay?"

The officers looked at each other and showed him the photo's they had taken.

"These marks are on your child's back. She has been badly beaten. Your nanny found them when your children were getting ready for bed and reported it straight away to your wife, who then phoned us to report it. Can you tell us where you were when this was happening sir?"

Kevin said he was with his children most of the time, apart from one day when he had to see some people in town.

"I was only away for about four hours as I had to get the train back home. Are you saying I did this to my child?"

"No sir, but we need to interview Shirley as she was the only person who was with the children, unless you have staff here?"

"No, I don't have any staff, but Shirley would never do this to a child."

"Can we talk to her sir, or would it be best to take her down to the station?"

"I'll get her for you."

"Sir, please don't say anything as it could affect our enquiries."

Shirley was interviewed and taken to the station where she was processed. The station inspector interviewed her for twenty-four hours. During the interview, she started to flirt with him and so a woman inspector had to join them in the room.

"Shirley, this is serious. You are accused of whipping a small child. What do you have to say for yourself?"

I did not do it. It must have been her mother."

"We did not say it was a girl, we just said a small child."

Shirley then went quiet. She was thinking about how could she get out of the mess.

"Kevin told me the children's mother was on medication for depression, so it must have been her."

Kevin was interviewed. He told the officers he had never said anything like that and that it was all false. His wife was not on medication for depression.

Shirley was arrested for beating a little child and was taken to court to be sentenced. She got thirty years without probation and her children had to be taken into care, as she was not married to their father and Sonya would not have them in her house. Kevin moved back home but the strain between him and Sonya was almost at the breaking point. She did not trust him anymore. When they were out together, she watched him like a hawk. If he looked at another woman he knew that a strong woman like Sonya would not take it on the chin. He had to dance to her tune from then on.

Sonya took the children out for a walk as it was a sunny day and she needed to get out of the house. At the shops she bumped into Mr and Mrs Wilson.

"Well hello there," Sonya said. "Mrs Wilson how are you?"

"We saw your husband a while back in a restaurant. He was with another woman. I forget her name."

"Oh that would have been Shirley," said Sonya. When the children were out of earshot Sonya told Mr and Mrs Wilson all about Shirley and what she had done to Mia.

"That is terrible. I hope you reported her to the police."

"I did and she is in prison for thirty years."

"I don't think that is long enough," said Mr Wilson. "Anyway if you need to talk to someone please call us and we will come straight over."

"Thank you," said Sonya. "We will speak soon. How about you both come over for drinks one evening next week?"

Mrs Wilson said. "Friday is good for us how about seven o'clock."

"Great," said Sonya. "I am looking forward to it, see you both then."

Kevin and Sonya had a heart-to-heart talk about his behaviour. He said that he regretted everything and promised not to wander ever again. He asked if they could go on a long holiday as a family.

"I am sure the children would love a beach holiday. We will ask them in the morning I am sure they will say yes."

The child protection officers wanted to speak to Kevin about Christine and Andrew as their mother was in prison they were placed into foster care and now there was a couple who wanted to adopt the children. Kevin was not expecting this but after talking it through with Sonya, he decided it was in the best interest for the children, as it would allow them to have a stable life and he agreed to them being adopted. The officers did tell him that he could not have any contact with the children, which was hard for him to comprehend but it had to be done.

Kevin asked the chauffeur to get the car ready for their holiday. "The nanny will be coming with us and there is a two-bedroom cottage for you both and our cottage is next door."

"Yes, My Lord," said Mr Parr. "What time do you want to leave?"

"About ten o'clock in the morning."

"That's fine, we will be ready sir."

The children were up early they were already packed but then Graham remembered he had not packed any books. Running upstairs, he ran into his bedroom to find two children standing near the window.

"Who are you and what are you doing in my room?" he asked.

"I am Christine and this is my brother Andrew. We have come to live here with our father."

"Who is your father?" Graham asked.

"Our father is your father."

"What!" said Graham and with that he turned and shouted to his mother to come quick.

Sonya and Kevin ran upstairs to find the children in Graham's room.

"How did you get here?" Kevin asked.

"We ran away. We don't want to go and live with that couple. We want to live here with you Daddy."

Sonya looked at Kevin and asked. "How did you know where we lived? Have you bought them here before?"

"Only once," said Kevin, "when I knew you were out."

"That's it! Get them out of here and phone the child protection officers. They are not staying here."

Kevin phoned the officers and told them to collect the children.

As they were being driven away Christine and Andrew were crying. Even Kevin had a tear in his eye.

The children's new family had to move away and make a new start. Their new school was close to their home, and they soon made friends. Kevin missed them and he had to keep it to himself so as not to upset Sonya.

Their holiday in the cottages was perfect and they all had a wonderful time. The children went swimming in the sea and Kevin and Sonya managed to spend some time together. The nanny and the chauffeur had time away and were able to do their own thing. They were now heading back home. The journey took a long time as they had to take a diversion; but at least the children kept themselves busy by playing I spy.

At home, the cook prepared the evening meal when the phone rang. It was the Wilsons asking if they could come over at eight o'clock for drinks. The cook said she would pass the message to Her Ladyship when they got in. As promised, Cook told Her

Ladyship about the phone call and Sonya called them back to say it would be fine.

The conversation that evening was the newspaper headline about Shirley. It said that the police were investigating to find out whether she had abused any other children. They wanted to speak to another family who had complained to the police when they found marks on their child's back after Shirley had babysat for them. At that time, nothing was done but the report was still on file. Kevin did not know what to say.

"You never know what a person is like or what they are capable of doing but beating any child or hitting them with your hand or slipper is not on. Well that is the end of that," said Sonya. "Let's change the subject."

As the years went by the children were growing up fast. Graham had asked Kevin if he could join the air force.

"What brought that on?" Kevin asked.

"Well I have been reading books on flying and I want to go into the air force."

"We will look into it," said Kevin, "but first, you have to get some rest, so off to bed."

"Good night everyone."

"Good night son, see you in the morning."

Graham was going to be leaving school soon. He asked his dad if they could visit an air force base. He had heard that there was an open day there. They took a trip to the base where they were met by the captain. After looking around and getting plenty of information Graham decided to ask the captain how soon he could enlist.

The Captain said. "Well son if you do want to join us you have to be seventeen and decide what you want to do like learning to fly or be an engineer, a chef, a medic or anything. Think about it, read up on it and then decide, if it's for you then come and enlist."

Graham said. "Thank you, sir, I will."

On the journey home everyone was quiet. Graham was thinking what he could do. He really wanted to fly but he needed a back-up plan. After thinking for a while, he thought that he would make a good medic. Both of his sisters had a few years at school still. Linda wanted to be a travel agent and Paulette wanted to be a nurse. Mia was too young and was still having home schooling. Kevin and Sonya wanted Graham to stay close to home but he was determined to enlist and when the time came they had to let him go.

He was not allowed home for two months, but when he was, he came home in full uniform. Looking very smart he marched up to the front door carrying his rucksack over his shoulder. Ringing the doorbell, he hoped his mother would answer but when the door opened it was Mia standing there. Her eyes were big and she had tears in them. Graham put his finger to his lips and stepped into the house. He gave Mia a big hug and kissed her on the cheek.

Mia said. "Mummy and Daddy are in the lounge having coffee."

Putting his bag down he took off his cap and went into the lounge. On opening the door, his parents looked up and saw this very handsome chap in uniform standing there. His mother got up and hugged and kissed him for ages, then she stepped back to have a good look at him.

"You've got so tall and broad. They must be feeding you well?"

"They are Mum. How are things here; are you both keeping well?"

"We are fine son," said Kevin.

He heard the girls running downstairs and entering the lounge they started to scream with excitement. Graham hugged them all. Cook had done a lovely lunch for them all, and then Mia asked Graham how long was he able to stay for.

"I am on leave for two weeks, so we have plenty of time to catch up with all you are doing. How are your lessons? Is Miss Evens giving you plenty of homework?"

"She makes me read a book each week, and then she asks me what the story was about. I told her it would be better if she read the book herself." They all laughed.

Graham told his parents he was training to be a pilot. He had started a couple of weeks ago and the captain said he was a natural. When he got back to base they would start in a flight simulator. He had passed his exams and eye test, and he said that the other recruits were great to be with.

Chapter Two

Linda left school and went to work at the local travel agent. At first, she thought the boss was a bit grumpy but it turned out that he was a friend of Shirley's, and he had determined that it was her mother who had reported her to the police. Linda found this out when she was getting a drink in the staffroom. Some of the other women were talking about it when Linda walked in.

Walking up to them Linda said. "Who can sit back and let this woman get away with whipping a little child? Mia had marks all over her back, so my mother had no choice but to report it to the police. Now, they are looking into other children she might have whipped."

Her boss did not know about this. He thought Shirley was a very kind woman. He said he had known her for quite a few years, Linda asked him if Shirley had ever asked him for money.

"The first day we met she did say she had to find her rent money or she would be evicted from her flat. I could not find the amount she wanted and I told her so. The next week she said she was being evicted as her landlord had found other tenants and she had to get out by the weekend. I told her to ask her parents if she could move back home for a while, but that did not go down well. The next I heard from her was that she had found a very generous man who had found a room for her in a hotel and that they were going to get married and start a family."

Linda was shocked to hear it. When, she got home after work she mentioned it to her parents. Sonya said that Shirley was insane and she must have been planning it all along, that was why she got pregnant; she wanted to marry a wealthy man, but it back-fired and she ended up in prison. "Let's hope she never gets out."

The next news from the prison was that Shirley had had an affair with one of the prison officers and was pregnant again. She hoped to be let out of prison to give birth, but that would not happen. As soon as she had given birth the baby would be taken away and put up for adoption. The prison officer had lost his job and had moved away. His family was devastated and was unable to contact him again.

Paulette was leaving school the next year. Nursing was her choice of job. She loved science at school, and that was a subject she had to take. She started to help out at the local nursing home on weekends and got on with both the staff and the residents. The sister asked if she wanted to work more hours in the school holidays. Paulette wanted to say yes straight away but she had to ask her parents first.

Her parents said. "If that is what you want to do, then yes you have our blessing and thank you Paulette for asking us first."

When she was at the nursing home the following week she told the sister she would love to do more hours.

"Thank you for letting me know Paulette. I shall put you on the roster and let you know the dates and times you will work. Do you want to do the same hours each week or will you be flexible?"

"Flexible will be okay," and with that Paulette went to take meals to the residents who had their meals in their rooms.

Mia had grown into a lovely girl. She had long eyelashes and dark brown hair, and the most natural curls anyone could wish for. Her mother said to her father that she could be a model.

"We will have to wait and see what she would like to do. She has plenty of time." Her father did not want his little girl to leave home just yet. Her school was pleased with the progress she made, and she had plenty of friends. She was a very popular girl.

None of her teachers at the school knew about her early years, so she was pleased to not have to explain to anyone what had happened, and then one of the parents who picked up their child saw Mia and recognised her from the newspapers. The whispering started, and at the end of the week every child in the school knew what had happened.

Mia's closest friends stayed by her side as their parents said, "It was not Mia's fault she was beaten. It was that awful woman who did it and she deserves all that comes her way."

Sonya walked around the garden and found a rosebush that Mr Hebden had planted under the nursery window. It was in full bloom and the perfume in the air was so strong that it attracted bees. Looking more closely at the flowers, Sonya picked a rose and put it in her hair, and then turning around, she noticed Kevin looking at her.

"How beautiful you are and that rose makes your face shine like it's under a spotlight."

"If you keep talking like that you'll make me blush," said Sonya. They walked arm in arm around the garden until the cook came out with a jug of freshly made lemonade and two glasses.

Putting them down on the table near the sun loungers, cook said. "Lunch will be ready in an hour My Lady."

"Thank you, Mrs Richardson. I think we will have our lunch out here. It's such a lovely day and why not make the most of the sunshine."

Arriving home after school, Mia told her parents that a parent who had picked up their child had recognised her and had started to tell all the other parents.

Mia said. "You could see everyone was whispering." Her closest friends had stayed by her side and the teacher had told the class that they should not listen to gossip. Before Mia left for home the teacher asked if what she had heard was true.

"Yes that evil woman did beat me and now she is in prison for thirty years,"

You poor child, now that it is out no more talk about it will be allowed in school."

Thank you Miss it would be good not to have to explain it every day to people."

Mr Parr was cleaning the car when Mia went outside and asked him if he could take her to the shops on the weekend as it was her parents' anniversary. She wanted to get something really nice.

"Yes Miss it would be my pleasure. What time would you like to leave, and do you know what shop you are thinking of, as there are plenty of shops in the town. Think about what you want to buy and we will then decide which direction to go in." Mia wrote a list and thought that her mother would like a bracelet and her father would like a new wallet.

That Saturday, Mia was up and dressed, put on her hat and shoes and told her parents she was going to town with Mr Parr and would not be long. As she ran down the driveway to the car Mr Parr held the door open for her. Climbing into the back seat, Mia said she knew what she wanted to get and told Mr Parr so he could decide where to go.

The town was very busy, so, having parked the car, he escorted Mia to the shops. Looking into the jewellery window Mia saw the most beautiful bracelet. Entering the shop Mr Parr asked the shop assistant if they could look at the bracelet in the window. Mia put it around her wrist to see if it was the one, and then looked at the price.

"That is perfect," said Mia. "Can you wrap it up for me please." Looking around the shop, Mia saw some leather wallets.

The shopkeeper said. "We can emboss it with the family crest if you would like, at no extra cost and it can be done straight away."

Mia said that would make it really special; so, after choosing the wallet and having it embossed with the family crest the shop assistant wrapped them up too, and after paying and saying thank you to both the shop keeper and his assistant they left and headed back to the car.

Driving home, Mr Parr said he hoped Mia had had a lovely time.

"Yes thank you. It was so good of you to come with me. It won't be long before we must start Christmas shopping then we can do it again." Mia had a smile on her face as she felt so grown up going out shopping with the chauffeur.

Shirley was talking to another inmate about what she had done, and to her surprise, the woman had done the same thing to her boyfriend's little girl, she even went a bit further and locked her in the cellar.

"Not for long," said the woman. Her boyfriend used to put the tin of shoe cleaning things on the top step, and she had moved the tin to the bottom and asked the girl to go and bring the tin up. "When she got to the bottom of the steps I turned the light off and locked the door." After a short time, she let the girl out and said, "Oh the door must have got locked by itself." She then told her if she ever told anyone she would be locked in for longer.

"Why would you do a thing like that?" Shirley asked.

The woman said. "She reminded me of her mother, and I hated her."

Shirley said she used to beat her boyfriend's child because she did not want to look after her. "If I could have killed her and got away with it, I would have. He has three other children and I like them because they are older, but this little girl needed attention and I was not willing to give it as I have two children with her father and they take all my time. They come first not that child, but this one will be adopted as soon as it is born."

Kevin and Sonya went to Graham's passing out parade. He passed with flying colours and was now flying jets all over the country. He had met the captain's daughter when they were at dinner and had asked her out. Kevin and Sonya had booked a table at the local hotel for the six of them, the Captain and Mrs Jones, and their daughter Sally. The evening went well and the meal was perfect. Sonya asked Sally what work she did. Sally said she was a doctor at a local hospital. She worked in the children's ward.

"How rewarding that must be." Sonya mentioned that their daughter Paulette was training to be a nurse and that when she qualified, she wanted to train to be a midwife.

Graham said he had three sisters.

Mrs. Jones asked. "What work are they doing?"

Kevin said. "Linda is working as a travel agent and Mia is still at school. We are not sure what Mia wants to do, but she has plenty of time to decide."

Captain Stephen and his wife Mary were talking about going on a cruise. They had not been on one before so they were looking forward to going on one.

"Where are you thinking of going?"

"Oh we are thinking of going around the Indian Ocean, but we may try a shorter cruise first just to see if we like it."

Mary asked Sonya if they had been on a cruise. "No we have never discussed it but maybe we should."

"Well if you do then we should go together; the four of us. What do you think Stephen?"

"Yes that would be great. At least then we'll know someone."

Arriving home, Kevin mentioned to Sonya that maybe Linda could look into it. "We will ask her when she gets home," said Sonya.

The next day Linda bought home some brochures on cruises for her parents to look through. Sonya said they were thinking of going on a short cruise to see if they liked it. "If all goes well we may book a longer one with Stephen and Mary around the Indian Ocean.

"Wow, said Linda, "you are pushing the boat out. If you choose which cruise you want to go on then I can give you a discount."

"Are you sure that would be okay with your boss?"

"Yes, he said that could be done; no problem there!"

Chapter Three

Sonya and Kevin arranged to meet Stephen and Mary at the travel agents the week after. Looking at the poster on the wall, Mary said, "Stephen what do you think. How about going to Scotland? There is a cruise that sails around the top of Scotland and goes to all the little islands then down to the south of England and then back home. It takes two weeks."

"That should be perfect. Let's have a word with Linda and see what she can do for us."

Linda put their details into the computer and there was plenty of room on board the ship. "You can have two double rooms or two suites. What would you like Mum?"

Sonya replied. "The suites sound good. What do they have in them?"

"They have a queen size bed, a bathroom, a sitting room with a large TV. Your baggage will be collected from the train and put into your room. Also, you have your own porter so if you want anything at any time of the day or night just ring the bell, and they will come to your room."

"That sounds perfect darling. Should we book it Kevin?"

Kevin asked Stephen and Mary if the cruise was good for them.

"Yes," said Stephen. "We have our passports here so we can book it right away."

Linda put their details into the computer and entered the date when they were going, and then she put her parents' details in.

"That's all done. Would you like to pay now, or should I send the bill three weeks before you sail?"

"No, we will pay now darling."

"Okay, Mum," said Linda. Her dad came to the counter and paid his bill then and then Stephen paid his bill. Looking at the paperwork, Stephen saw the name at the top of the paper and read the name Lord and Lady Swan. His eyes nearly popped out of his head. He never mentioned it to Kevin and Sonya but when he got back home he could not wait to tell Mary what he had read.

"Did you know that they are Lord and Lady Swan?"

"What!" Said Mary. "Lord and Lady Swan. No I had no idea. I just thought they were a down-to-earth family."

"Well I am glad we did not know as this would have put us into a tricky position when their son became a pilot."

"What has that got to do with their son being a pilot."

"Some people will think we gave him his wings because of his parents' title."

"Nonsense," said Mary. "He was at the top of his class on his own merits and that had nothing to do with his parents."

"Yes we know that, but some people may have other agendas."

The three weeks went by so fast. They only had a week before they would be sailing around England. Sonya started to pack her cases, making sure that she had plenty of dresses and shoes to match, and a new evening outfit for when they were sitting at the captain's table. Stephen and Mary were organising things at their end and had to find someone to look after their dog while they were away.

The big day came and Kevin asked their chauffeur to drive to Stephen and Mary's home to pick them up so that they could all be together on the train. Arriving at their home, Mr Parr got out of the car and rang the doorbell saying to Mary that His Lordship was in the car waiting to take them to the station.

"We will be right with you," Mary answered.

So, putting the suitcases in the car and opening the car door for Mr Mrs Jones to climb in Mr Parr started driving towards the station.

Mary said. "This is a nice surprise. We did not know we would be driven in such a lovely car."

"Well, we are going to the same place so why not," replied Kevin.

Their porter was waiting for them to arrive at the station and they made their way to the first class carriage where they had a glass of champagne The carriage was almost empty but it was pure luxury. Mary had never travelled that way before. They normally travelled like everyone else in 'the cattle lorry,' her husband used to say. The train journey was about four hours long so the porter came and asked if they would like some food. He had brought them a menu so, after choosing, they had a hot meal and some more champagne.

Arriving at the station to board the ship, the porter got their luggage and had it delivered to their cabin. The captain welcomed them aboard and told a crew member to take them to their cabins so they could freshen up before having drinks on the top deck. So, walking to their suites, Mary said to Sonya. "We will call on you when we are ready, I think we will need a rest first as we were up early this morning."

"Okay," said Kevin. He turned to the porter and asked, "What time will we be meeting the captain for drinks?"

"At seven o'clock sir. I will come to you and show you where to go. I will let you relax now. Is there anything I can do for you sir."

"No thank you," said Sonya. "We are fine, see you at seven."

The porter left them to rest and headed back towards the staff quarters. He did not have to see to any other passengers just Lord and Lady Swan, and Stephen and Mary's porter had to do the same. The two porters were friends and had both worked in hotels, so they were used to looking after VIP's.

At seven there was a knock at the door, so Kevin went to answer it. It was the porters to take them up to the top deck for drinks, just behind them were Stephen and Mary.

"How is your suite? Do you have everything you need?"

"Yes thank you. We even have a bottle of champaign and a large basket of fresh fruit."

"That's good. We have the same," said Sonya.

The captain was talking to some other guests and when they entered the room, the captain turned to look at them, made an excuse, and walked towards them.

Kissing the ladies' hands, he said. "Welcome! please help yourself to some champagne. We have some nibbles too."

The captain wanted to talk to Kevin so they walked over to the windows. The captain started to say it was his pleasure to have a lord and lady on his ship.

Kevin said. "Please, we don't need special treatment. Just treat us like any other passenger."

"We will but it is a treat having a lord and lady with us, not every ship can boast that."

Their first stop was in the west of Scotland, where they could get off the ship for a couple of hours and have a guided tour. Mary enjoyed it and she even managed to buy some souvenirs. Kevin had whisky, and Sonya had bought some tartan to make the girls kilts. After two hours they headed back to the ship where the captain was waiting to greet them. Their porters took their bags to their rooms, while the captain had drinks ready on the top deck.

"We will sail further north and in the morning you could get off on an island."

Shirley went into labour, after forty-six hours the doctor said. "If the baby is not born today we will have to intervene and take the baby out."

Shirley did not want that to happen and she started to become angry. "The doctor said that if you don't calm down we will have to sedate you and strap you to the bed." Hearing that she calmed down and did what they told her. Her labour went on for another four hours and then she gave birth to a little boy. He was taken away and put into a cot. Shirley never got to see him or hold him. When the child services came to take him away they asked what his name was so that it could be written down on his records.

The doctor said. "His name is William and his weight is seven pounds two ounces." The doctor had not asked Shirley what

31

she wanted him to be called so he gave the boy his name. That way he would start his life with a clean slate. He had new parents waiting for him back at the office, and when he handed the baby over to them it was a perfect photo.

The girls at home had a whale of a time. Mia was taken to and from school each day by Mr Parr. Linda was working hard at the travel agents, and Paulette was doing long hours at the nursing home. They each received a letter from Graham telling them how he was doing and what sort of plane he was flying. He mentioned that he would be coming home in two weeks for three weeks and would be bringing a girlfriend to meet mum and dad. The girls got excited about this news so they started to plan things. Their mum and dad would be home from their cruise soon and they wanted to determine how it had gone.

Mr Parr went to the station to pick up Kevin and Sonya. Mia wanted to go with him, but he said that he would be dropping Mr and Mrs Jones at their home, and with the luggage, there would not be enough room. Mia went back into the house with a face as long as a fiddle. She soon recovered as she could not be angry with anyone for too long. Mrs Richardson was baking some cookies, which smelt delicious. The aroma went all around the house, which made everyone feel hungry.

"Are they for when mum and dad get home?" Mia asked.

"Yes but if you would like to be my taster you can try one for me."

Mia could not wait she washed her hands then sat at the table tucking into a cookie. There was not a crumb left on the plate.

She then said to Mrs Richardson. "They are okay, but if I must give marks out of ten then I must have another one."

"You cheeky lass," said Mrs Richardson with a big smile on her face. "You can have another one when your parents are here."

Mia heard the car pull up in the driveway and ran out to greet her parents, giving them both a big hug, she asked them if they had a lovely holiday.

"We have darling thank you."

As they went inside they could smell the cookies then Mrs Richardson said. "Shall I bring coffee into the lounge, My Lady?"

"Yes please, Mrs Richardson."

Mia followed her into the kitchen, brought the plate of cookies into the lounge and placed it on the table.

"Where are your sisters, Mia?" Sonya asked.

"Linda had to go to work, and Paulette was at the nursing home. They are home this evening."

After opening the post Kevin gave a letter to Sonya it was from Graham, it read that he was coming home with a girlfriend and would be there for three weeks. Sonya's face lit up with excitement and she asked Mrs Richardson to get some extra food in as they would have visitors for three weeks.

The following day Graham arrived with Sally. The whole family was pleased to see them. Mia showed Sally to her room that was next to her room, then they went into the garden and had coffee and cake. Kevin asked Graham how things were going at the base. He said that he was enjoying it and was flying some big jets. Graham could not take the smile off his face when he announced that he was engaged to Sally. He had asked her father for her hand in marriage and he said yes.

"Congratulations to you both," said Kevin.

Sonya shed tears of happiness and gave them both a hug. The girls were asked if they would be bridesmaids – a big yes came from all of them. Graham took Sally to see her parents. Her mum was busy in the kitchen. She made coffee and they all sat down in the lounge discussing the wedding date and what would be the best time of the year for it.

"A summer wedding is nice as there are a wide verity of flowers then, but it depends on you two and which time of year you are aiming for."

Sally said. "Next year would give us plenty of time to organise things."

"Then we will have to go wedding dress shopping, and you both have to decide where you want to get married and have the reception."

Graham wanted to talk it through with his parents, so they arranged to get everyone together during the three weeks he was home.

The girls looked through fashion books and wondered what sort of dress the bridesmaid could wear, that would be in fashion.

"Perhaps you should wait until they decide on the colour scheme first," said Sonya.

"We can have them made for us Mum," said Linda, "in whatever colour we decide."

"That's okay. Now let's go downstairs and have some lunch."

The church was booked and Sonya and Mary started to design invitations.

Kevin said. "The printers will talk you through it; they know what will be best."

The next day Sally, Mary and Sonya went to a bridal shop to have a look at dresses.

The assistant said. "Do you have any idea what sort of dress you would like?"

Sally said she liked the dress to have either short sleeves or thin straps. The assistant went into the back and came out with a dress that had thin straps that came into the waist and then flared out, the other dress was with short sleeves and flared from the bust line. Sally tried them on and thought the second one was not quite right, her mother and Sonya agreed, saying that it just didn't feel right

After changing into the first dress, Sally came out of the change room. "Wow! You look amazing."

Sally said. "This is the one."

The assistant then got some veils; first a short one and then a long one.

"The long one looks better," said Sonya. "Are you going to have flowers in your hair or would you like to wear a tiara?"

Sally looked at Sonya hoping she will be able to wear the same diamond tiara that Sonya had worn for her wedding to Kevin. Sonya saw the look, then offered her the tiara.

"It would be my pleasure if you would wear my tiara," said Sonya.

"Well that's sorted," said Mary. "Leave the dress here and then you can come in closer to the date and have any alterations done that are needed."

On the way home Sonya asked if Mary and Stephen would like to come over for a meal in the evening.

Mary replied. "Thank you, that would be lovely."

"Should we say about six then we can have a drink first."

The girls came running out to greet them.

"Have you chosen one," said Mia.

"Yes and it looks fantastic."

"Where is it I want to see it."

"We have left it at the shop, so it can be altered if necessary."

After lunch, Sonya asked Kevin if he could get her tiara out of the safe as Sally wanted to wear it on her wedding day.

"Yes but it hasn't been taken out for years, so do you want to try it on first."

Sonya and Kevin went upstairs to get the tiara. Looking in the mirror Sonya tried it on. It sparkled in the sunshine. Kevin looked at her and remembered their wedding day.

The three weeks went by so quickly but at least they had been able to get everything done in time. Saying goodbye to Graham was hard on Sonya. She never knew how long he would be away for. The girls kept her busy and Mia enjoyed having her mother to herself when Linda and Paulette were at work.

One weekend Mia asked Mrs Richardson if she could help in the kitchen. She replied. "You can decide what you want to make."

"Well it will almost be coffee time and mum and dad liked the cookies I made the other week."

"That would be helpful but do you still remember how to make them?"

"Yes I think so, but if I forget you can remind me."

Mia got the mixing bowl out of the cupboard with the rolling pin, cutters and the scales and then went into the pantry to get the flour, sugar, butter, and chocolate chips.

"There I think I have everything," she said and started to make the cookies.

Mrs Richardson looked over at Mia and asked. "Do you have a baking tray to put the cookies on?"

Mia looked at her with a big smile and said. "I knew I would forget something."

Passing a baking tray to Mia, Mrs Richardson said. "You can't remember everything but you are doing well."

The cookies were just about to go into the oven when Mia thought she would make a special one for Mrs Richardson. She made one that had a big smile made out of chocolate chips, then putting the tray in the oven Mia closed the oven door and put the timer on. The smell of cookies wafted around the house making Sonya and Kevin feel hungry. The coffee was on the tray and Mia placed the cookies on a plate. She put the cookie she had made for Mrs Richardson on a plate and left it in the kitchen. Carrying the plate of cookies into the lounge Mia put it on the table. Her dad asked who had made them. Mia replied that she had, without any help.

"I think these are the best cookies I have ever tasted," said Sonya.

"I want to cook other things if you will allow me to learn from Mrs Richardson. I promise not to get in her way." Sonya said she would ask Mrs Richardson first, and, with that, they sat talking about all sorts of things.

Paulette was at the nursing college taking an exam. Her tutor was impressed with her progress. After the exam was over she approached Paulette and mentioned that there was an opening in the maternity ward at the prison.

"The pay is good and you can choose how many days you want to work."

This came as a big shock to Paulette as she knew Shirley was there and she did not want to come face to face with her.

"Can I let you know after I have thought about it. This is something I must discuss with my parents."

Her tutor thought this was strange but said. "Yes, let me know what you decide as soon as possible so then I can offer it to someone else if you turn it down."

That evening Paulette mentioned it to her parents. Kevin said it was up to her. If it made her uncomfortable, she should decline the offer and go with her gut.

The next morning Sonya asked Paulette what she had decided. "I think I would prefer to work in a hospital than in a prison."

"Well that has answered the question. Are you going to tell your tutor today?"

"Yes; she has other nurses who would be perfect for the job."

Paulette met with her tutor at lunch and declined the job at the prison. "I would like to work in a hospital or even do home births."

The tutor asked her if she minded telling her the reason why she did not want to work in the prison. At first Paulette was reluctant to say anything but then she thought she would tell her about Shirley.

"I remember reading about it in the paper so that was the woman who whipped a child on her back with a belt."

"Yes, it was my little sister my parents don't know but she also hit me with her hand across my face several times because I had dropped some crumbs on the table when I was taking my plate to the kitchen."

The tutor asked. "Why did you not mention that to your parents?"

"She threatened me with more punishment if I said anything to anyone so I had to keep quiet, I know she had another baby in prison that was taken away so she never got to see it or hold it. I know it is not nice but I am glad it was taken from her. She lost the other two children she had and they have been adopted and the family has had to move away."

"I understand said the tutor and I am sorry about this, I shall see if there are any jobs going at the hospital and will let you know."

"Thank you," said Paulette.

When lunch was over Paulette had to go to the nursing home and do the night shift. She handed in her notice as she was a qualified nurse and was only being paid a minimal wage, but she thanked the staff for helping her through the hard times. They all wished her well in her career and promised to keep in touch.

Paulette's new job was at the hospital on the maternity ward. The matron was a young African lady, named Brenda who took Paulette under her wing and they became good friends.

One day, Brenda asked Paulette if she wanted to become her second in command.

"I have only been here for a few months. Don't you think the other nurses would be better for the job? I don't want to tread on their toes."

"The job has been advertised on the notice board for months and we have had no takers."

"I will consider it and let you know if that is okay?"

"Yes that's fine. I don't think there will be a rush for the position."

Paulette told her parents about the offer and they were pleased for her. They both thought it would be perfect and having a midwife in the family and a future doctor! What else could they wish for.

Mia had decided to become a chef as she loved cooking and baking and Mrs Richardson was a great help. She decided to enrol at the college. At first she did night classes. She was then offered a place in class during the day. Mia loved it she was getting really good at cooking. The teacher asked her if she could help out at a dinner party for the navy.

"What do you want me to make?"

"We need someone to make a four tier cake representing the navy. Do you think you can do it? We need it for the twentieth of December, which is four months away."

Mia replied. "Yes I would love to do it. Will I have help with it or do I have to do it on my own?"

"You will have help but it is up to you what design you choose, so I would get a sketch book and start sketching your design. Who would you like to help you out. We have Jean who is good at baking and Rose who is good at icing."

Mia said. "Yes they both work hard and know what they are doing."

"Great! I shall get you all together in a classroom on your own and you can get started. It must be ready a couple of days before as we must make sure the icing is dry."

Mia got together with Jean and Rose and started to sketch a four tiar cake. Rose had some good ideas on the design she thought to have a ship on the top of the cake with flags and waves around the edge.

Jean said. "How about a cake shaped like a ship instead of a round or square cake."

Mia started to sketch a ship-shaped cake, which looked fantastic. "The decoration of the waves could go around the bottom while the flags go on the top. Let's think about it for a day or two and meet up again with some designs." They all agreed, and Jean and Rose took their sketch books and went home.

Mia mentioned it to Mrs Richardson to see what she thought. "I do have some photos of ships and you could find some designs of flags. I am sure your father must have a book or two in the library."

"What a good idea. I shall have a look thank you chef," said Mia with a smile on her face.

Chapter Four

Sally and Graham's wedding day was approaching fast; only two weeks before the big day was here. The bridesmaid's dresses were chosen and the fittings were booked for the following week, Sonya and Kevin had nothing to do as the bride's parents had everything in hand, Sonya asked Mary if they had been back to where the reception was being held to make sure that everything was going to plan. "Yes," said Mary, "everything is going to plan and they have the drinks and food sorted so you don't have to worry – just enjoy the day."

Mia was in her room looking through the books from the library making notes of the flags that would be on a ship. She sketched different types of ships some with guns, some with helicopter pads and planes and one with loads of sailors standing all in a line just like they do when they first set sail. When she went back to class she asked her teacher which ship she thought the navy would like and what the dinner was in aid of. It was the admiral's final voyage, as he would be retiring at the end of the year.

"I think the ship with all the sailors standing around the edge would be perfect."

"Can you tell me his name as I think I can put it on the ship; maybe in flags."

"His name is Admiral Anthony Clark." And with that, Mia met with Jean and Rose.

She showed them her designs and they both agreed with her that the one with the sailors and the flags would be perfect. Mia asked Rose if she could start on the flags that would spell out the admiral's name and they would all start making the little sailors first, as she thought they would need hundreds of them.

Mia had to stop working on the cake as she had to concentrate on her brother's wedding, getting ready to go for the fitting. She was glad that she was not making their wedding cake. The dress was perfect. It did not need altering. Her mother asked what jewellery she would be wearing.

"I have a small pair of earrings and a gold chain with a gold bracelet do you think that is enough?" "Yes, you don't need too much."

Mia asked Sally what she was going to wear in her hair to hold the veil on. Sonya said. "I have offered her my tiara; the one I wore when I married your father, it is perfect and when you and your sisters get married then you can wear it. I will show it to you when we get back home."

The big day had arrived Graham was in his room making sure he had everything when his father walked in holding a small box.

"Today is your wedding day and I have had this made for you to wear. Then in time, you can pass it down to your son on his wedding day."

Graham opened it and looked at his dad with tears in his eyes.

"It's lovely Dad thank you." Graham put the watch on. Looking at the watch he noticed that it bore the family crest. He gave his dad a big hug and said he would only wear it on special occasions.

"I don't think my mates would appreciate me wearing something like this at work. Well, let's go downstairs and have a drink before we get ready."

The girls were having their hair and makeup done and their nails painted. Sonya had done her nails the night before and went into her bedroom to get the tiara out of the safe. It was in its red velvet box and she asked Kevin to go and give it to Sally and she asked him to tell her that it had to be returned later that day before they went away on honeymoon.

Mr Parr drove Kevin back home where the girls were already in their dresses; and they all had a flower in their hair. Sonya said they must have a photo taken before setting off for the church and they asked Mr Parr to do the honours. His hands were shaking a bit but the photo turned out fine.

"Another one for the album," said Kevin.

The church was full of guests when the girls arrived. Mia walked down the aisle first, followed by Paulette and then Linda; each carrying a small bouquet of flowers. Sitting by his mother and father he waited for Sally to arrive, Graham looked at them all and mouthed *you all look lovely.* Then the vicar asked everyone to stand. *Here comes the bride* was being played and then Mia saw Sally walking down the aisle. The tiara sparkled in the sunshine and her dad was so proud. He was dressed in his air force uniform with the braids and medals on his chest and a sword on his left leg.

Arriving at the altar, Graham turned to look at Sally. "Hello, you look beautiful."

"Thank you," said Sally.

After the vicar did his job he then said to Graham. "You may kiss the bride."

All the guests started to cheer and then they went into the vestry to sign the register and have photos taken. Outside, the guests were talking and getting the confetti ready for when the bride and groom came out. Confetti went everywhere. All the family had bits in their hair. Arriving at the reception, the guests sat at their tables and waited for the bride and groom.

Then the best man said. "Ladies and gentlemen, please welcome the new Mr and Mrs Swan."

Sitting at the bride and grooms table were Sally's parents, the best man, the bridesmaids, Graham's parents and of course Graham and Sally.

After it was all over, Kevin, Sonya and the girls headed back home. Mr Parr was waiting for them in the car. The drive home was full of love and laughter. Once inside the house they were met by Mrs Richardson who asked if it had gone okay.

"It was perfect," said Kevin. "We will be in the lounge if anyone wants us,"

Kevin had just started to pour a glass of whisky for himself and a glass of wine for Sonya when the front doorbell rang. Mr Parr opened the front door and was faced with a man in uniform. At first, he thought he was from the airforce but it was a policeman.

He asked if His Lordship was home and said he needed to have a word with him as it was very important. Mr Parr asked him to step inside and went to fetch Kevin. Kevin asked what the problem was and took the policeman into his study so they could speak in private.

"Sorry to disturb you sir; we have some bad news. We believe you know a woman named Shirley who was in prison?"

"Yes, said Kevin. "Why what has happened is she dead?"

"No sir she has escaped and has taken her daughter Christine, who we believe to be your daughter as a hostage."

"Where did this happen?"

"She escaped a couple of days ago, grabbed your daughter and is now on the run. She is armed and dangerous. She left a note saying she wanted to talk to you or she would kill your daughter. We think she may call you here and therefore we must ask whether it will be okay for us to set up a phone tap so we can listen in."

"Yes that will be okay. Do you really think she would kill Christine."

"Yes sir we cannot take any chances and Christine is a child."

"Let me tell everyone here what has happened while you set up the tap on the phone."

The doors were locked and everyone had to be on alert, because if they saw any movement in the gardens they had to report it to the police. Kevin said Shirley would not phone him at home, but could arrive at the house so they had several offices posted inside and outside their home. That night, Kevin and Sonya could not relax. They spent most of the night talking about the wedding and then Sonya remembered that her tiara was not back in the safe.

"Never mind said Kevin I am sure it is safe. We will send Mr Parr to the Jones's house to collect it in the morning."

The front doorbell rang, and one of the offices answered it. There, standing with a knife to her daughter's neck stood Shirley, and behind her were two officers who had seen her coming to the house. They had kept their distance so as not to scare her.

"I want to speak to Kevin," demanded Shirley.

The officer said he would get him. Kevin came to the door saw his daughter with a knife at her throat. He asked Shirley what she wanted.

"I want some money and a home for me and our children.If you don't do what I ask I shall kill Christine here, right now."

Christine was crying and she begged her father to do what her mother wanted. The two policemen outside came closer and Shirley told them to back off or they would be sorry. Kevin tried to persuade Shirley to stop what she was doing but her mind was made up. He then realised that she had lost the plot and told her that he would not give in to blackmail. He walked away hoping she would not go ahead with her threat.

Christine shouted. "Daddy please don't turn your back on us we need you."

Looking over his shoulder, he saw Christine walking towards him and he realised she was in on it.

The two policemen arrested Shirley and Christine and said that they would be taken to the court the next day, where Shirley would have her sentence extended and Christine would have to go into child custody, knowing that her mother had done this to her. Shirley would be locked away for a very long time. Christine was not sorry and told the judge that they had planned the whole thing when she went to visit her mother. Christine got ten years.

The judge said. "You will not be out before your ten years are up. You will not be able to have visitors and when you are released you will have to report to the local police station every week."

Shirley's son Andrew was happy with his new family and was an ace student. He was not told what his mother had done and that his sister had been locked away for ten years. The court had kept his name out of the papers, so no one knew he was the son of this woman.

At the weekend while the family were having dinner the conversation was about the punishment Christine had been given.

Sonya said she deserved all that the judge gave her. It was the only way she would learn and with some help she might be able to turn her life around. Paulette then mentioned that Shirley had slapped her across the face when they had been to visit the few days years ago.

Kevin asked. "Why did she hit you?"

"It was all because when I took my plate to the kitchen some crumbs fell off onto the table. She lost it and hit me several times across the face, and then said that if I told anyone I would get more the next time."

"Why did you not say anything earlier?" Sonya asked.

"I still thought she would get to me and now that I am older I know she can't do anything to me."

"My poor child, you had to keep this from us all this time. Well, at least she is locked away for what she did to Mia."

Mia did not know what they were talking about as she was too young to realise the danger she was in.

Back at college, Mia was baking the cake for the admiral's party. It was going to be so big that she had to ask the woodwork teacher if one of the students could make a large cake board that had to be large enough to put the cake on and wide enough so the decorations would not fall off. It needed to be ready in a few days as she had to carve the shape of the ship.

"Yes, we will get right on to it; and thank you for thinking of us," said the teacher. "I will let you know when it is ready."

The phone rang and a voice on the other end said. "Hello is that the Swan family residence?"

"Yes," said Mrs Richardson. "Can I help you?"

"Yes can you tell me if Mr Swan is in?"

"Yes, he is. May I ask who is calling?"

The voice said. "It's Richard Swan."

"Thank you, I will go and tell him."

A few seconds later Kevin came to the phone and said. "Hello, this is Kevin Swan how can I help you?"

The voice answered. "Hello Dad it's me, Richard." Kevin had to sit down it was a shock to hear his name. "Dad are you still there?"

"Yes," said Kevin. "How did you find me?"

"I saw your photo in the paper. It was a photo of your son's wedding."

"Oh yes! and how do I know you are my son? Who is your mother?"

"My mother is Carol. You met her at a dance in 1930 and I was born nine months later. She always told me about you. When I was old enough, she told me to find you. She knew you had two other children and was married when we saw your photo in the paper. I knew I had to get in touch, do you think we could meet up for coffee? I can get on a train and come to you or we can meet in a pub or park I don't mind which."

"We had better meet in the park, so how about Wednesday say, at about three o'clock?"

"That's fine. I am looking forward to meeting you."

Ending the call, Kevin had to tell Sonya that he had another son. He remembered Carol but had no idea they had a son together.

That Wednesday, Kevin was sitting on a bench reading the newspaper when he heard someone approaching him. He looked up to see a young man; well dressed in a Royal Navy uniform.

Richard said, "Hello, I am Richard, are you Kevin?"

"Yes," said Kevin, standing up. They shook hands. "Should we go for a walk?"

They walked for quite a long time and asked each other loads of questions. It turned out that Richard had been in the navy for quite a few years and had recently been appointed Admiral of the British fleet; who would be taking over when the current admiral retired at the end of the year.

"Well, that is good news! My daughter Mia is making the cake for his party. She will be pleased to find out her half-brother is going to be the new admiral."

"When can I meet her and the rest of the family? I only have three weeks off before I have to report for duty."

"How about tonight? Come for dinner, say about six. Everyone should be home then."

"That sounds good. My last train leaves at ten."

"If you miss that train you can stay the night. We have room."

"Thank you, but before you go can I have your address?"

"Of course." Kevin wrote it on the top of the newspaper and handed it to him.

"See you at six. It's been good meeting you," said Kevin.

At six the front doorbell rang. Mr Parr answered it and standing there was Richard.

"Please come in His Lordship is expecting you."

Richard thought to himself. *His Lordship, have I got the right house?* Richard was asked to follow Mr Parr to the lounge where the family were having a drink before dinner.

Entering the room, his father stood up to greet him. "Hello son, please come in and meet the family. This is my wife Sonya and these are your half-sisters Mia, Paulette and Linda. Your half-brother Graham is on honeymoon so you will meet him soon I hope."

"Pleased to meet you all," said Richard. Kevin asked if he would like a drink. "Thank you," said Richard. "Do you have a beer?"

Mia laughed and said. "We have everything."

Passing a beer to Richard, Kevin said. "Come and join us, dinner won't be long."

The evening was going well, but then Richard said he had to go and get his train home.

"When will we see you again?" Sonya asked.

"I have three weeks leave, so I am sure we will meet up again soon."

"Take care son; give us a call when you are free."

"Thank you all for a wonderful evening," Richard said.

"Mr Parr will take you to the station," said Kevin.

Mr Parr was waiting in the car. Driving to the station, Richard asked Mr Parr about His Lordship. Not knowing if he should answer or give away too much information, he kept it brief and said he had been working for the Swans for many years and that the whole family were kind to their staff.

"That's good," said Richard. "I have been on ships for many years and you soon get to know the crew though some do swap ships from time to time."

It was almost Christmas and the cake was done. The decoration was perfect; all ready for the party. Two of the ship's crew pushed the trolley with the cake on it into the hall where the admiral and his wife stood talking to the mayor. As the guests arrived, they all went to have a look at the cake.

"How lovely," said Mrs Clark. "That must have taken ages to plan. Can we meet the chef who made it?"

"Yes," said the mayor. "She is here."

Mia went over to have a talk with the admiral and his wife.

"Have you been doing this job for long?"

"No sir. This is the first large cake I have made and hopefully it won't be the last."

"I am sure you will be in demand now," said Mrs Clark.

"The mayor said you have family members in the forces. Is that true?" the Admiral asked.

"Yes, sir. I have one brother who is in the air force and another one in the navy."

"Oh, what is his name – the one in the navy."

"Richard; he has been promoted to admiral and will be taking over his new post at the end of the year."

"Richard Swan?" said the admiral.

"Yes sir," said Mia. "Do you know him?"

"I do; he will be taking over from me."

His wife said. "Well, what a small world."

Christmas day arrived and the whole family were together apart from Richard who was at sea. He did, however, manage to phone his mother and then his father to wish them all a merry Christmas, Sonya and the girls went to church in the morning and then back to a lavish dinner, all cooked by Mrs Richardson. The staff were always invited to have Christmas dinner with the family. No one worked that day so Kevin and Sonya did the clearing up and the girls made sure that their glasses were topped up. After the dinner was over they started to open their presents. The rule was that no one spent more than ten pounds on a gift, so the person who got the cheapest gift was the winner. The gifts included a scarf, driving gloves, a note pad, a plastic ring, a pack of tissues, a lipstick and a pack of wooden spoons, the winner was Sonya who got the pack of tissues.

Graham and Sally had been married for several months when they got a dog. They lived on the base so when they were both at work a dog walker came to take the dog out for his daily walk. Graham loved to train the dog in the evening. He got him to sit by his leg and stay until he was told to walk. One day Graham took him out and they came across a squirrel running across the grass. His dog which they named Jack stayed by his master while another dog chased the squirrel up a tree. Graham praised Jack for staying and gave him a treat, and after a long walk and a bit of training on the field they headed home. Graham told Sally what Jack had done. He was so proud of him for staying by his side.

Sally gave him a big hug and said. "Good boy Jack."

A few months later Sally thought she might be pregnant but kept it to herself until she had a test done. She was in good health, but somehow felt different; so getting on with life and putting it to the back of her mind, she suddenly felt a little faint at work. She had to sit down and one of her colleagues came over and asked if she was okay. A little while later, her colleague asked if she could be pregnant.

"I think I might be but I've not had a test done yet," said Sally.

After she had had a test, Sally went to the toilet to look at the test. She saw the answer she had been waiting for. She was pregnant. She made an appointment to see her doctor. Went home to tell Graham the good news.

When Graham got home from work Sally said. "You had better sit down as I have some news." Graham looked startled. At first, he thought the news was that his father or mother were ill.

"No!" said Sally, "it's just that you are going to be a father. I had a test done today and I've booked an appointment with the doctor for next week.

The following week, Sally went to see the doctor who confirmed the pregnancy. The due date was next summer, after waiting three months before telling anyone, Graham and Sally went over to his parents to give them the good news.

"Congratulations," came from the whole family and staff.

Mia asked if she could take Jack for a walk around the estate. Graham said he would go with them as he needed to show Mia what training he was doing with Jack; and he did not want him to pick up any bad habits. They started to walk but Graham made Jack sit by his side before they set off.

"He is very good at taking orders from you," said Mia.

"Yes, we do some training every day and he is very good at not running off or chasing squirrels as we have a lot of squirrels on base; so, very soon you will be able to take him out on your own, as long as we keep up with the training. "

"I promise to keep up with the training when you come over."

Sally and Graham went over to see her parents before returning to base. They were pleased to hear that they were going to be grandparents. Mary started to get some knitting patterns out and ordered some wool from a shop in town; and before long, she was knitting away, making a baby outfit and blankets for the new arrival.

Kevin and Sonya were out in the garden talking to Mr Hebden. He was looking at the rose bush that was planted under the nursery window when Mia was born. It still had lovely roses and the aroma was strong.

"We were thinking of getting another rose bush when our grandchild is born. Do you think you can look into it for us Mr Hebden?"

"Yes My Lord. I have a catalogue at home and I will bring it in tomorrow for you to have a look at." "Thank you," said Sonya.

The land around the estate was vast. Most of it was lawn with a few flower beds and trees. There was a summer house in the garden, where Sonya liked to have her afternoon tea, Mary Jones came around one day while Sonya was in the summerhouse reading her book. They chattered for ages about the garden and who did what on the base. Sonya would have said that it was gossip and she was not interested in gossip, but she had to look as if she were interested. Kevin came out to see if Sonya was okay. He knew that Mary had been there for some time and he thought that Sonya wanted to be rescued.

"Oh, is that the time? I have to go," said Mary. "Stephen will be wondering where I am."

"Bye," said Kevin as he took Sonya by the hand and led her inside for dinner.

Chapter Five

Graham phoned his parents to say that Sally was in hospital. "It looks as though the baby is coming sooner than was expected." Her labour pains started in the early hours, he was with her and was asked to step outside while they looked to see how far things were progressing. Kevin asked to be kept informed when the baby was born and asked Graham to give Sally their love.

The girls were excited to be aunties, but they had no idea what sex the baby would be. Mia said she thought it would be a girl but Paulette said. "No, it's going to be a boy," as Sally was carrying it high. A few hours later the phone rang, and they all jumped to attention, with smiles on their faces, Kevin answered it.

The voice on the other end said. "Hello Granddad." Graham announced that he was a father to a beautiful baby boy. His name was Kai, and he weighed seven and a half pounds. Mother and baby were doing fine, and congratulations came down the phone line.

"We are so proud of you," said Kevin. "The girls want to know when can they visit the baby."

Graham said. "Not today as Sally wants to get some rest, but come tomorrow. I will find out the visiting times and let you know."

Sonya could not get over being a grandmother. Kevin asked her what she wanted to be called grandmother, granny, grandmama or nana. Sonya thought for a while and then said. "Nana I think."

Then congratulations nana on your first grandson.

Sonya was putting Kai's name on the blanket she had made. She commented to Kevin on what a lovely name Kai was. "I wonder where they got that from." Kevin agreed it was unusual and then said, "Kai Swan, it sure has a nice ring to it!"

When Sally and Kai left the hospital they went round to Kevin and Sonya's home so that everyone could meet Kai. The staff swooned over him. They had all chipped in to buy a baby rattle. It had four little silver bells and a mother of pearl ring at the bottom. It was very special, the girls all had a cuddle and then he was handed to Sonya for her to have a cuddle. Kevin asked Mr Parr to take a photo of the whole family, and after it was taken, he said. "Another one for the album."

Graham took his family home so Kai could have a feed and be put down in his cot for a sleep. Some of the families at the base wanted to go and see little Kai, so Graham asked a few of them to come the next day, so as to not have too many people in the house at once. After everyone had seen him, Sally's parents came to the house for their cuddles.

"He is gorgeous," said Mary. She asked how his first night at home had been.

"He slept for six hours," said Sally. "I was awake thinking he wanted his feed, but when I went to him he was fast asleep."

As time passed in the Swan household, the girls had grown up and Mia had qualified as a chef and worked in a hotel, but in her heart she wanted to join the navy and work on a ship. After discussing it with her parents, she got the forms and filled them in. Posting them, she got butterflies in her stomach. She said she should hear from them soon, and then she would hand in her notice. Linda was the manager at the travel agents; and she had been all over the world. She loved to travel and said that the long-haul flights were the best. She went first class now and again, as many of her customers were gentry and only wanted the best. On one flight, one of the crew saw her in the queue and asked if she would like to board early and have a look in the cockpit.

"Thank you," said Linda. She felt very special. The captain was in his seat checking through the paperwork. It would be a while before the rest of the passengers were on board. The captain asked her name and she answered. "Linda Swan."

He then asked. "Do you have a brother called Graham?"

"Yes why?"

"I used to work with him in the Royal Air Force (RAF). He was my captain and we flew very fast jets; and then I got a job working for this airline."

"What a small world it is," said Linda. "Now you are flying me to Australia."

The rest of the passengers were on board and Linda had to take her seat. The captain said he would come and talk to her once they had taken off. After half an hour, the drinks came round and Linda had a glass of champagne. Looking through the menu, she decided to have lobster, then beef wellington, followed by chocolate sponge pudding and ice cream. The captain came and sat down on the seat next to Linda. He was young and very good looking.

"Hello, I am sorry I did not introduce myself earlier. I am Phillip Peterson. How are you? and do you have everything you need for your flight?"

"Yes, thank you I am fine." Linda asked him how long he had been working for the airline.

"Oh, two years now. I mostly do long haul flights. Tell me how is Graham? Is he still in the RAF?"

"Yes, he is still at the same base with his family. He is a dad now to a lovely boy called Kai who is almost one, and is the apple of his dad's eye."

"That's good, and are you married?" the Captain asked.

"No," Linda replied. "I am the manager of the local travel agency and I have to travel to discover the best places for my customers to go to on holiday."

"So, would you recommend this company to fly with?"

"I am sure it will go down well with my customers because they like to be spoilt."

Just before they were due to arrive in Australia, Phillip came back to see Linda. He asked if they could meet up and have a meal. He told Linda where he was staying and asked for her phone number so he could keep in touch.

After a couple of days, he phoned Linda and they went out to a lovely hotel for a meal. They met up several times during their trip to oz; and arriving back home they kept in touch, although Phillip did have to fly off more often than he wanted to.

Arriving back home, Linda spent the evening with her parents talking about her trip and telling them about Phillip; and about how he knew Graham from when they used to work together on the base flying jets.

"Well, he sounds nice," said Sonya. "When are you going to see him again?"

"When he gets back," she replied. "He is on his way to America. He will be away for two weeks." The living room door opened and in walked Mia. She had been baking cookies; her dad's favourite.

"Oh, my little angel has made me cookies. This is the best time of the day. We need some hot chocolate to go with these."

"It's on the way," said Mia. Then Mrs Richardson walked in with a tray full of cups and a large jug of hot chocolate.

News had got out that Shirley was getting out of prison but that she would have a tag on her leg. She would have to report to the local police station every week and would have to be at home from six p.m. to nine a.m. every day. She would not be allowed anywhere near Lord and Lady Swan or any of their family. She was put in protective custody with a female officer every night. She did not like the thought of being held prisoner and she wanted to visit Kevin; but that was out of the question. Luckily, the house did not have a phone so she could not phone him. After she had been out for two weeks she found out that one of his daughters was the manager of the travel agency in the town and she had tried to go there to speak to her. When she got close to the travel agents she was spotted by an off duty officer who phoned the police station and they sent a squad car to pick her up. Screeching to a halt outside the shop, two officers got out of their car and escorted her into the vehicle. The bystanders wondered what had just happened. Soon after, she was back at the safe house with another female officer and was kept under house arrest for the remainder of the week. Gossip went around the town about the woman who not many people knew about, but when they found out the truth, she was the most hated woman ever and some of the residents tried to get her run out of town but that was not likely to happen.

Paulette was on duty at a home near her parents. A lady near-by was about to give birth to her first baby and the labour was progressing nicely. Paulette said she had time to have a bath if she wanted, as that would probably help her with the pain and would definitely relax her. While the bath was running, Paulette got some warm towels out of the airing cupboard and; looking out of the window she spotted someone in the garden next door. *I thought the house next door was empty thought Paulette.* As far as Paulette was aware, the house had not been sold, and yet she had seen someone; probably a woman in the garden.

After Paulette got the lady in the bath she left her to have a soak for a while and went into the garden to see if she could see the woman. She spotted her through the hole in the fence and recognised her straight away.

"She is supposed to be in prison," Paulette said in a whisper to herself it was not that quiet.

Shirley looked up and walked over to the fence.

"Hello who is there," she said.

Paulette did not know what to do. She tried to walk into the house without Shirley seeing her, but it was too late.

Shirley shouted. "Paulette is that you? I have been trying to get in touch with your father."

"He wants nothing to do with you. You whipped my sister; you are a nasty woman and should be in prison."

"I am out and living here and you can't do anything about it."

Paulette was so angry that she walked over to the fence where she saw Shirley standing on something to look over the fence.

"I can do something about you living here, you just wait!"

With that, Shirley swung her arm and hit Paulette in the face. Blood poured from Paulette's nose and Paulette knew Shirley had broken it. Running inside to get a towel, she picked up the phone to call for help; first for the other midwife to help with the delivery and then the police. When the officers arrived, Paulette reported the assault and they went round to arrest Shirley and take her to the station. Paulette went to hospital to have her nose checked out. It was broken and she was told to rest for the next couple of days. The neighbour delivered a healthy baby boy weighing seven pounds three ounces.

Shirley was taken back to court where the judge told her that she would be going back to prison as she was a risk to people in the area. He added another six months to her sentence. The events were reported in the newspaper where the headline said; *woman out on bail breaks the nose of a midwife*. Paulette stayed at home for the next few days as the bruising on her face subsided. Kevin felt sorry for her and regretted ever getting involved with Shirley.

Kevin and Sonya went to see Kai. He was growing up so fast; he loved lying on the floor with his mobile over him playing a tune. As soon as he saw Kevin and Sonya he started to kick his feet and gave the loudest squeal and the biggest smile you could ever see. Sonya picked him up to have a cuddle but he wanted to go to grandad. Kevin was as pleased as punch to have the little mite in his arms.

Sally said. "He is going to be grandad's little darling."

Sure enough when he had to be put down in his cot he cried until grandad gave him a kiss, and then he went to sleep. Having a cup of tea in the lounge Sally asked how Paulette was. "Oh she is fine; a broken nose will not keep Paulette down for long. Her bruising is going down. It looks like she's had ten rounds in a boxing ring."

Sally said. "She could have it reset in hospital; it's a simple procedure and she will only be in hospital for a couple of nights."

Sonya said she would put it to her when they got home.

"So, how are things with you both? Do you get to see your parents much?"

"Dad is working a few days a week on base and mum is looking forward to him retiring. She is planning to take him on a cruise, as they loved the last one they did with you two."

Driving home that afternoon, Kevin asked Sonya if she wanted to go on holiday. "It's been ages since we went away and I could do with some time away."

"Yes; where to?"

"I'm not sure. I fancy a long flight to somewhere hot."

"Okay, let's have a look when we get home. I fancy India, but we will have to be careful not to get a bad stomach; or even Thailand. I hear it's a wonderful country."

Kevin was getting excited about the trip so Sonya had to make sure she kept him grounded for the time being; otherwise he would be running off to the travel agents booking a holiday.

After the girls got home, they sat and had their evening meal. Kevin told them that they were thinking about going and having a holiday somewhere hot. Linda told them the best place to go at the moment was Thailand but it was the rainy season. You'll get more *bang for your bucks* now. If you want I can bring some brochures home tomorrow for you to look through."

"Thank you darling, that would be great!"

Mia had a big announcement to tell the family. She had been accepted by the navy and would be a head chef on board one of their ships.

"I cannot tell you the name of the ship yet, but I will be leaving in three weeks, so if you and Dad do book a holiday you don't have to postpone it because of me."

"But darling, we want to see you off. We cannot go away and not see you off on your travels. You will have a great adventure out at sea; visiting loads of countries."

"I will Mum but I don't want loads of fuss."

"You are our baby and we will miss you but we know you have a calling to the sea; and you will have a big job to do, feeding all those sailors. Anyway, we have three weeks together, so let's make it special."

The days went by so fast and Mia only had one week left with her family. She spent hours walking around the shops with her mum and bought plenty of toiletries. "There is no need to buy dresses and shoes as I will be working or resting," said Mia.

Her mum gave her a big hug. "I will miss you but the only thing I want you to do for me is to phone us when you can."

"I will, I aim to call at least once a week as I know you will want to hear what I have been up to, and I will want to know what is happening here."

Arriving home with all the shopping bags, Mia went to her room to pack her case. Her dad called her to come downstairs as there was someone to see her. Running downstairs as fast as she could, Mia ran into the lounge and there standing in front of the fire was a man in uniform. As he turned round towards her Mia gave a big smile. It was Admiral Anthony Clark. He had come to tell her the name of the ship she would be on.

"It's the *Royal Outlander* and I believe there is someone on board you know very well."

Mia started to think, and said, "I don't know anyone on board sir; are you sure about this?"

"Yes, it's Richard your brother."

Mia smiled. "Well, at least I'll have someone to chat to when we are off duty."

Kevin was pleased about this, as he knew Richard would look after Mia.

Mrs Richardson came in with some coffee and homemade cookies. The admiral sat on the sofa and Mia sat next to him. She wanted to know what she should do when she arrived at the ship the following week.

"Don't worry about that; I have organised someone to be with you to show you the ropes and they will be with you for the first month. If you have any problems at all, they will help you."

"That is very kind of you," said Kevin. "I cannot believe my little girl is leaving home."

"We will take good care of her and before you know it, she will be home on leave."

Admiral Clark had his driver outside waiting with the car. He had been ordered to take the admiral back to base as soon as possible; so; upon ringing the doorbell and waiting on the steps, the door was opened by Mr Parr. He said that he had an important message for the admiral.

"Please come in," he said. They are in the lounge."

Entering the room, Mr Parr said to Kevin. "The admiral's driver has a message for the admiral."

The driver said he had been ordered to get the admiral back to base.

"Thank you, I will be with you in a minute. I am sorry I have to cut this visit short, but be assured, I will make sure that Mia is kept safe at all times."

"Thank you," said Sonya.

"We look forward to your next visit," Mia said and went to the front door to see the admiral off. Shaking his hand, she said she looked forward to the next week and getting to work in the galley.

"Goodbye my dear, see you soon."

Sonya was speaking to Mrs Richardson in the kitchen. They were planning a small dinner party for Mia before she left.

"We will need to keep it quiet and hope that she doesn't find out. The dinner will be on Saturday so she can recover on Sunday before she leaves on Monday."

"Leave it to me," said Mrs Richardson. "I will sort it out. How many people are you inviting?"

"I think there will be about twenty, but we will confirm the numbers closer to the weekend."

Mia sat in the lounge reading. It was a lovely summer's day. The birds were singing in the garden when there was a crashing sound in the hallway. Mia got up to investigate; and there, standing among a heap of toys was Kai.

"He wanted to see his auntie," said Graham. "So we had to bring his toys to show you."

Mia replied. "What a lovely surprise! come in and let's play."

Kia showed Mia his new toy. It was a big blue boat. "This is your boat you will be on, Auntie Mia."

"It is," said Mia. "You are a very clever boy."

"Daddy said you go on Monday to cook for some sailors on your ship."

"I am doing that, but it won't be long before I am home again for a holiday."

"Will you give me a call when you are coming home so I can come and play again."

"I will darling."

Just then, Kevin and Sonya came into the room.

Kia shouted. "Granddad, Nana, come play. I have a new toy. It's a blue boat the one auntie Mia is going to work on."

"Wow," said Kevin. "That looks fantastic! Will you put it in the bath?"

"No Granddad it's too big." They all laughed.

"Bless him," said Sonya.

Then her thoughts went to Mia, when Shirley had whipped her. Kevin knew she was thinking about Mia and the woman who had whipped her. He regretted ever meeting her. She had had a hold over him and wanted to be the new Lady Swan; but that would never happen. He wondered what his two children were doing, but he could not get in touch with them. He had his and Sonya's children to think of. They came first and now that Kia was here, he had his hands full.

Chapter Six

The day of departure had arrived. Mia was excited to get to the ship, as well as sad about leaving her family. Her bags were put into the car and everyone was standing on the steps with tears running down their faces. Sonya was shaking. She did not want her baby to go.

"I will be okay Mum. I have Richard to look after me. Mia kissed everyone and gave a big hug to Kia. "See you all soon," she said. With that, she climbed into the car and Mr Parr drove her to the station. Unloading her luggage, Mr Parr said, "Good luck to you miss Mia, and if you visit any exotic countries send us a postcard."

"I will and thank you for being a good friend, bye."

The train journey was long and hot even though the windows were open. Mia got her notebook out and started to invent some recipes without even noticing that more passengers had gotten on the train. An old couple sitting at the next table looked at her and whispering. Mia lifted her head and glanced over.

"Can I help you," said Mia.

"No, we are fine. We were just thinking you look very much like someone we used to know."

"Oh, and who would that be?"

"A little girl who used to come to a house near to where we lived. Her dad had a girlfriend and now she is in prison. We don't know why but she did something bad and you look like the child who played in the garden."

"Well, I am sorry to say, yes I am that child and as far as I am concerned she can rot in prison for the rest of her life."

The couple could not apologise enough. They felt so sorry for bringing the subject up.

"Never mind you were not to know." Changing the subject, Mia asked if they were going to visit family.

"No, we are having a few days away; a mini-break you might call it."

"That sounds good."

"So, where are you off to? Are you going to meet your boyfriend."

"No," said Mia. "I am joining the navy and will be cooking some lovely meals for the crew."

Wow! What an adventure. Will you be visiting different countries?"

"Yes, but I have to get my *sea legs* first."

The train started to slow down. Mia could see the station and said that it was her stop.

As she started to get her things together the old lady grabbed her arm. "Take care love. Whatever that woman did, she is in the best place for people like her."

Mia said. "Have a nice mini-break and take care, Bye!"

Stepping off the train and gathering her luggage together, she felt a hand on her back. Looking around, she was surprised to see Richard in uniform with a big smile. "Well, hello Sis," said Richard.

Mia threw her arms around his neck and they were both hugging each other for what seemed ages. People were looking at them as they walked by, and some of the women said. "How lovely."

"What are you doing here," Mia asked.

"I have come to help you get to the ship I was not going to let a total stranger collect you and your luggage, so I had a word with the admiral for permission to come myself, and here I am."

The car waited just outside the station to take them to the ship. The journey was short but for Mia, it was wonderful to see Richard again.

"Just one thing I must say," he said. "When we are on board we cannot hug each other, as I am the second in command. We have to respect the rules."

"That's fine. I understand but we can get to see each other when we are off duty can't we?"

"Yes, that is allowed. Well, here we are. Let's get you on board and I will introduce you to the person who is going to stay by your side for the next month. She is about your age and has been with the ship for about two years. Her name is Amy and she is one of the sous chefs, so you will be seeing her most days."

The ship was on the grand scale. Amy took Mia to her cabin so she could drop off her luggage and then she took her to the mess, so she could have a drink and meet some of the crew she would be working with. The galley had everything they needed, so Mia was eager to get started. She had a meeting with the head chef. He was a very big man who had to squeeze past the row of ovens.

"Hello Miss Swan or may I call you Mia?"

"Yes please, call me Mia."

"Have you worked on a ship before?"

"No, this is my first."

"Well, we run a tight ship here. We work hard and play hard, so to speak. You are on duty for twelve hours a day, and the first thing you do in the morning is to get everything ready for the main meal of the day. We eat our main meal at seven p.m. after the crew and even the admiral. Then after that, you can relax and the rest of the time is yours. Do you have any new recipes you think we could try?"

"Yes, I have quite a few."

"Then can you run them by me, and then we could make a few dishes and see if the crew likes them." "Sure! I have a portfolio in my cabin and on my way here on the train I wrote some new recipes."

"Well Mia, I think you are going to be an asset to us. Go and rest and we will catch up tomorrow."

The next day, Mia got up early. She was a bit wobbly at first as it was the first time she had been on a ship; so, walking down to the galley, she had to hold on to the grab rail. Amy caught up to her as she was about to go the wrong way.

"Go this way or you will be late starting work and we don't want chef getting angry do we?"

"No, we don't, and thank you it's going to take me some time to get my sea legs and find my way around the ship."

"To help you, there are signs on the walls above the fire escapes at the end of every corridor so you will soon get to know your way around the ship."

The chef was waiting for Mia to arrive.

"Do you have your portfolio with the recipes?"

"Yes, they are here." Mia showed the chef and he seemed impressed with what she had done.

"We will get straight on to it."

Some of the kitchen staff were willing to help. After a couple of hours there were heaps of dishes and Mia had made stacks of cookies. She knew that they would go down well with the crew so she made sure she saved some to give to Richard.

The weeks went by so fast and Mia had no idea what the date was or the month, for that matter. The ship's captain called her to his office. He wanted to see how she was getting on and he asked her if she had any problems.

"No sir; I have made loads of friends and I love working in the galley. Sometimes, I like to cook some of my new recipes and try them out on the crew. They seem to like them which is nice."

He said. "I have called you in to see me Miss Swan as I have some bad news for you. I received a call from your father, saying that your mother has been taken ill. She is in hospital and they are not sure how much longer she has, so your father asked if you could be put on compassionate leave. I have agreed for you to go home and come back when you feel the time is right."

"Thank you sir. I shall get my things together. Can you tell me whether you have told Richard?"

"No, I thought you would like to tell him. If he wants to go with you then that is fine. We can cope until you are both back."

"One more thing sir? How do we get off this ship when we are so far from land."

"There is a helicopter waiting on standby, so go and get yourself ready; and Miss Swan; we hope your mother improves."

"Thank you sir."

Mia and Richard were on the helicopter flying home, and the pilot was able to land in one of the fields close to the house. As they climbed out of the helicopter Kevin ran to see who it was. When he saw it was Mia and Richard both in uniform, he thought his heart was going to burst!

"My darling!" he shouted. "You have come home. He flung his arms around Mia and then Richard. "Come on in. I shall get Mrs Richardson to make us a hot drink. Oh where are my manners? please come and join us for a drink. Your helicopter will be safe here."

"Thank you sir."

As they entered the house, Richard introduced the pilot to his father. "Dad, this is Stephen. He is one of our crew and he flies the helicopter whenever he gets the chance."

"Come on in. I am so glad you were able to get my children back home safe."

Mrs Richardson came in and placed a large tray on the table. As she poured the tea and placed the cookies on the coffee table, she said to Mia. "It is good to see her again."

Mia gave her a big hug. "It's good to see you too, we will catch up later after we have seen Mum."

Stephen said he had to get back to the ship before he became AWOL.

"Well, thank you again," said Kevin.

Mia and Richard said they would send a message when they returned, and wished the pilot a safe journey to the ship. "See you soon."

Arriving at the hospital, Mia asked which room her mother was in.

"Lady Swan is in room one. She is resting at the moment, so if you would like to come back later, I will tell her you came."

Thankfully, Mia was still in her uniform. She felt she had more power when she was in uniform, and she said to the nurse. "I have left a ship out at sea to fly here to see my mother, and I am not leaving until I have seen her."

The nurse was taken aback. "I shall see if Lady Swan will see you."

"Don't bother. My mother will see me now." With that, Mia walked into her mother's room as soon as Sonya saw it was Mia she started to cry. "Don't cry. I am here. How are you feeling? What happened and what do the doctors say is wrong with you?"

"All these questions! Let me look at you first, you look so nice in your uniform. I am okay darling. The doctors say that my heart has been playing up so I have to take some medication to keep it in a good rhythm. I should be home soon. How did you know I was here."

"Dad phoned the ship and the captain told me and Richard to get home fast. We flew home by helicopter and landed in the grounds near the house."

"So, how long are you able to stay?"

"As long as it takes for you to get better."

Kevin was reading when Mia arrived home. She told her dad that her mum hoped to be home soon, and that she had told Mia that her heart was playing up and that as soon as they put her on the right treatment, she would be on the road to recovery.

"Is that what she told you? Well, the doctors had told a different story. They said she was poorly, that they had no idea how long she had left, and that maybe the family should get a specialist to see her." "That's a good idea," said Mia. "I will get on to it in the morning."

While Mia lay in bed, she could hear her dad and Richard talking in the lounge. They were discussing anything and everything. Her ears pricked up when her dad asked how Mia was coping with being away from home and being on a ship.

"She is doing very well," Richard said. "The captain said to me before we left that he was impressed with her ability to cope in the galley. I know it can get very hot in there and working under pressure can get to the best chefs after a while; but she loves it. She turns out some lovely meals and the whole crew like her. I can assure you if there was anything at all that was bothering her, I would know about it. After all, she is my little sister."

Chapter Seven

Sonya arrived home with strict orders to rest. The doctor wanted to see her in two weeks, so Mia had to get a specialist to see her before then. The date and time were booked for the following week, so Kevin got Mr Parr to drive them to the appointment. Mia sat in the car waiting for them to come out. The chauffeur was very chatty. He wanted to know how she was and if she loved cooking for all those crew members on the ship.

"Yes," she said. "They are a good bunch I have made loads of friends. even the captain keeps an eye on me. The worst thing was getting my sea legs. I had to hold onto the grab rail for weeks, but I am pleased I don't get seasick any more."

Lord and Lady Swan came out from seeing the specialist. They were all smiles and holding hands. Climbing into the car, Sonya said. "Thank you for getting that sorted for us darling, I have received the all clear."

"That is good news, so let's get home and have some lunch. I am feeling a bit hungry now."

Richard sent a message to the captain on the ship saying that all was well, and they would be reporting for duty within the next few days. That would give them both time to say their goodbyes and buy a few things that were needed.

The helicopter landed on the same spot, close to the house. Richard asked if all was well on board the ship.

"Yes sir," said Stephen."How are your family; all well I hope?"

"Yes, thank you," Richard said. "Would you like to come in and have a drink before we set off."

"Thank you, that would be nice."

Sonya was resting in the lounge when Richard and Stephen walked in.

Richard said. "This is Stephen our pilot and a member of our crew."

Stephen said. "Please don't get up My Lady, you need to rest. It's so good to see you and I am pleased you are on the mend."

"Well, thank you. Please sit down. Coffee will be here soon."

Mia was getting dressed in her uniform, ready for the flight back to the ship. Her bags were packed. She said goodbye to all the staff before having coffee with her parents.

Richard said. "We all have to get going. Take care My Lady and father; if you need us to get back quickly, let us know. We can fly back at short notice."

"Thank you son."

Mia gave her mother a big hug and a kiss.

Her father said. "Take care both of you. Thank you Stephen for bringing them to us and for taking them back. Fly safely."

Back on board, Richard and Mia reported to the captain and then went to their bunks and rested as they were not on duty until the next day. Mia sent her parents a message saying that they had arrived back safely.

Sonya found the house empty after Mia and Richard had left, but she looked forward to them coming home for Christmas, which was not that far off. Kevin started to plan for the Christmas family gathering. He ordered the turkey, got all the Christmas lights out and made sure that they were still working.

"We still have three weeks before we need to get the decorations up," said Sonya.

"I know darling, but we have to be prepared you never know what is going to happen within the next three weeks."

Sonya started to write her Christmas list for gifts, and then the food list. Before they knew it, three weeks had passed, the lights were up on the trees outside and the tree in the hallway was decorated. Kai had asked father Christmas for a train set; and he was running around the house like a train. "Steady on their lad, or you will crash into the tree," said Kevin.

"Granddad I am a safe driver. Just ask my dad. He tells me all the time that I am the best back seat driver EVER."

Mia and Richard arrived home for Christmas. They managed to get three weeks leave but did not tell Sonya or Kevin they were coming, as they wanted it to be a surprise; so on Christmas eve, they rang the front door bell just as Kevin was walking by. He opened it to find the two of them standing there with their luggage and a big sack full of gifts. He wanted to shout to Sonya but Mia shook her head; so after entering the hall, they walked into the lounge and put cold hands on Sonya's face, and then a big kiss on each cheek.

"Oh my darlings, you have come for Christmas. You did not let us know. We had no idea if you were able to make it or not."

"We are here Mum for three weeks. We have a sack of gifts for everyone. Can we put them by the fire in the corner?"

"Yes darling, that would be good."

The next day was Christmas day. Graham Sally and Kai were coming over for breakfast; then sometime later Linda and Phillip were due and then finally, Paulette would be there before lunch. That was a full house.

"Do you want me to make other plans," said Richard.

There was a loud. "No!" from everyone.

"You are staying here!"

Mia looked at him and said. "We are family but if you want you can put a tent up in the garden." They all laughed.

Sonya said. "Mia you are terrible."

Christmas day started off with a glass of champagne and one little boy standing in the lounge looking at all the presents in the corner.

"Wow! Father Christmas has been busy."

While everyone sat in front of the fire, Kai started to give the presents to everyone with the help of Richard, who read the labels.

"This one is for Kai," he said.

It was a very large box, so with a bit of help, he opened it, to find a train and carriages and loads of tracks.

His dad said. "I think we had better set that up after breakfast."

"But can I just have a look at the engine," said Kai.

"Okay," said Graham.

Kia got the engine out of the box and holding it tightly, he started to walk to the table for breakfast.

"That's a good boy."

Sally said. "Should we put it on the table, then,? After we have all eaten Daddy can set it up for you."

After breakfast, presents were opened and more drink was being poured into glasses. The whole family sat in the lounge talking about things and watched Kia playing with the train set.

"Granddad do you want to come and play with me. I will let you be the train driver."

"That is good of you," said Kevin, "but I think Daddy or Uncle Richard want to play with you. One can drive the train, while the other one can be the station master."

Both Graham and Richard looked at Kevin and said. "Thanks for that Dad."

Christmas dinner was perfect. Crackers were pulled and everyone wore their party hats, but just as Kai was going to tuck into his roast potatoes, his hat fell over his eyes. Kevin started to laugh because the poor chap couldn't see anything. His mum got hold of a paper clip and fixed it.

"There you are big boy," said Richard. "All fixed."

When the meal was over, Kai asked if he could leave the table and go and play with his toys.

"Yes darling," said Sonya. "We will be there soon."

When he had left the room, the topic got serious. Graham said he and Sally had some good news. They were expecting another baby in the summer. Then Linda announced that Phillip had asked her to marry him.

Paulette asked. "Did you say yes?"

"Of course, I did, and before you ask, we have not set a date."

"Well, I think this is a time to have a celebration drink," said Richard. "Cheers to the new arrival this summer; and another wedding. Does anyone else have any good news you want to share?" but no one said anything.

Mia was sitting in her room reading when there was a knock at the door.

"Come in," she said. When the door opened she saw someone standing in the shadows who she did not know. "Who are you and what do you want?"

The person did not say anything and just stood there. She was getting a bit scared at that point and so she shouted to Richard and Graham. They came running up the stairs and were faced with a man in a trench coat, hat and glasses.

"Who are you?" they said, "and how did you get in here."

The man did not speak but tried to push past them, but they managed to get hold of his arms and forced him against the wall.

Richard pulled off his glasses and asked. "Do you know him?"

"No," said Graham "I have never seen him before."

Just then Kevin came up the stairs to see what the commotion was and saw that Richard and Graham had a man pushed up against the wall.

He looked at the mans face. "Andrew, what are you doing here? How did you get here?"

Graham demanded. "Is Andrew the son you had with that woman Shirley."

"Yes," said Andrew. "I am your half-brother."

"That does not give you permission to come into our home and scare the living daylights out of us. We should call the police and have you arrested for breaking and entering."

"All I wanted was to see the girl my mother whipped and to say to her that I am sorry for what she did to her."

"Well, you went about it in the wrong way," said Kevin. "You are not welcome here so you had better leave before we call the police."

Graham wanted to throw him down the stairs, but Richard kept a strong grip on his arm. Getting to the front door he let go of him and said he was never to come back. Mr Parr was asked to make sure the intruder was off the property and was told to lock the gate.

Kevin went into the study to look at the CCTV. He saw that Andrew had jumped over the fence and worked his way into the house, through a window on the ground floor; the room next to where Kai was playing with his toys.

"That's it," he said. "I am going to get alarms fitted to every window in the house. I am not having my family put in danger."

Richard and Graham were in Mia's room talking about what had happened. She was still in shock. "How could he have gotten into the house and up to my room? For that matter, how did he know that I was in my room and which room was mine?" Things were going around in her mind. *He could have had a knife or a gun. stop thinking like that he has gone now and will never come back or he will be arrested.*

Graham agreed with Richard and said. "Dad must get better security from now on."

It's all right darling. I have looked at the security tape and he got in through the window next to where Kai is playing."

Graham asked. "Is Kai okay?"

Richard replied. "Yes he does not know what happened and is still playing with his toys."

"Thank goodness for that," said Mia. "Come on lets go and play with the little chap."

They all went into the lounge. Mia wanted to be the train driver this time.

"Auntie Mia are you okay?" said Kai.

"Yes darling, why?"

"Oh, I heard you call out to Daddy and uncle Richard."

"Oh that, yes it's all sorted now. Well, what are we going to play with now? How about the building blocks? Let's see if we can build a fort."

"That's a good idea," said Richard, as he got to his knees. "Come on Graham get down on the floor and start building. This is going to be the grandest fort ever."

The next day, Kevin walked around the estate's boundaries with Graham and Richard discussing where they needed new cameras. He said he would get alarms on every window and have spot lights fitted around the property, Graham said that it would look like Fort Knox.

"I don't mind as long as my family are safe. If that man can get into the grounds and house, then others can do the same." They all agreed that the security did need an upgrade.

Richard said. "You can always have it connected to the local police station, so if anyone does try to get in then they will be round like a shot."

"That sounds good. I will look into it. Thanks lads, and thank you both for your help. I am not sure I could have managed to get him out of the house on my own. We are lucky he was not armed; but anyway, where would we be but here for Christmas?"

A few days later Richard received a phone call from the captain of the *Royal Outlander* to say that the ship was heading back to port as it needed to have some major work done and most of the crew would be on leave for the next few months. He told Richard to tell Mia that they would have at least two months at home.

"Thank you sir," said Richard. The captain hung up.

Mia, as well as her parents were pleased that they would be staying on land for at least two months.

"Do you know what is wrong with the ship?" Mia asked.

"No," said Richard.

He only knew that they were heading back to port for some major work which would take at least two months. Kevin was pleased at least, he would have Richard to help with installing the new alarms around the house.

The work was going on all around the house. Floodlights were being put up around the property and alarms were fitted to every window. Kevin added all the alarms to the computer while the fitter mounted a large keypad on the wall in the hallway, and one in the master bedroom, and when the testing started, he asked Lady Swan if she would like to go outside as the bell would be very loud. Richard said he would stay with the fitter just to make sure things were safe. It took about half an hour. All was working well and then Kevin added the secret code. The workmen left, and Kevin told Sonya, and the rest of the family the code.

"Should we tell the staff the code?" Sonya asked.

It was decided that they would only do so when the time was right.

Chapter Eight

Spring was just around the corner. Some of the bulbs were pushing their heads through the last of the snow. Mr Hebden was busy in the greenhouse, planting seeds in trays and pots. He had the heater on as it was a bit nippy outside. Mrs Richardson came out with a hot cup of tea for him and a couple of cookies on a plate.

"Thank you very much my dear, but I could have come indoors."

"Never you mind," she replied. "I have just cleaned my kitchen floor and I don't need you walking in with those wellies." They both laughed. "So tell me, what are you planting there? Are they veg seeds for the raised beds?"

"Yes, and I am trying a few new ones, so when they start to grow I will let you know so you can cook some wonderful meals."

"Oh, you are a charmer Mr Hebden. When you have finished your tea, leave your mug and plate by the kitchen door."

Graham called at the house with Kai, and asked Mia if she would look after him as he was taking Sally to the hospital for a check-up. Kai was a lovely little boy; very kind and thoughtful, so after saying goodbye to his father, he said to Mia. "Can we play a game?"

"Yes, what do you like to play?"

"I like cards or a board game."

"Well, I think we have a game called 'sorry' have you played that?"

"No, but it sounds fun."

As Mia was getting it out of the games cupboard Kai was looking as he had never seen the games cupboard before.

"Wow Aunty Mia you do have a lot of games."

"They are not all mine. They belong to everyone, whenever we get a new game it is put in here."

"I think I will ask Daddy if we can have a games cupboard."

"I am sure he will sort one out for you."

That game of sorry went on for ages. Kai won most of the rounds. He could pick things up quickly and he never lost his temper if he lost. When his daddy and mummy came to collect him he was full of beans.

Running to them, he said. "I have been playing a game with Aunty Mia. It is called sorry and they have a games cupboard. Can we have a games cupboard Daddy?"

"Slow down lad, lets go and see Aunty Mia."

Mia was sitting at the table, putting away the game. Mia asked how things went as she could read the look on their faces.

"All is well," they said.

So they left it at that, as it was too soon to say anything to Kai.

"So, I hear you showed him the games cupboard."

"Yes, and he wants to know if you can make him one."

"Thanks for that, little sister."

Mia smiled. "Well, every child needs a games cupboard. That's how they get to keep their room tidy."

Sally agreed. "We do have a few games that are on top of the chest of drawers in his room."

Kevin and Sonya had been in town. They liked to have a day out together now and again. When they came into the lounge Kevin went over to the fire to get warm.

"It's still a bit chilly out there. I think we are going to have a frosty night."

Kai said. "Granddad, do you mean Jack Frost is coming tonight."

They all laughed. "Yes son, Jack Frost might come tonight."

Mrs Richardson came into the lounge to say that lunch was ready in the dining room, they all got up and went through. There was a good spread laid out; it was a cold buffet with a ham joint and beef with all the pickles and cheeses.

"Thank you, Mrs Richardson, it looks amazing," said Kevin.

Kai was hungry. He was ready for this but he waited until everyone was seated and his daddy had poured him a glass of water. No one spoke for quite a while, as they were enjoying the meal too much. Then Kevin gave a big burp and tried to blame Kai.

"Granddad it was not me," said Kai. He looked around the table to see everyone shaking their heads at Kevin.

"Sorry lad, that came up from my big toe."

"Your big toe?" said Kai, "that is so funny!"

Linda and Phillip came round that evening to discuss their wedding plans. They were planning a summer wedding and wanted to see what date was good for everyone. Mia said that she would fall in with whatever they decided, and Paulette said the same. The staff were good at the hospital, so no problem there. Graham and Sally said that as long as it was not too late in the summer, they should be fine. Richard did not say anything as he was not sure if he would be invited.

Linda asked. "How about you Richard. Are you okay with the summer?"

He was taken aback by the question. "Oh yes, I did not say anything as I did not know if I would be invited."

"Of course, you are invited, you are family."

"Then yes, summer sounds like a good time to have a wedding, if you need any help with arranging anything please let me know."

"Thank you," said Linda, "that is good of you to offer."

Paulette had a few days off so she and Mia had a girl's day out, they went shopping and had coffee and cake in the town's best coffee shop. They talked about everything from work to the latest fashions, magazines, to boys, Mia said she had not laughed so much in ages.

"It's great having a day out with you. I miss our little catch ups and it's not great that I am out at sea for months on end."

"Are you saying you want to leave the navy?" Paulette asked.

"No, not at all. I love it but I do miss you all."

"Ah, that's homesickness; you will get over it when you are back on board the ship," Paulette said.

"I hope so," replied Mia.

"Maybe we can have a video call once a week. Let's make it on a weekend. I shall send you a message first to see if it's a good time."

"Yes that will work."

Richard walked out of the house when the girls arrived home with their bags of goodies.

"Let me help you with those."

Taking their bags and placing them in the house, he turned to Mia and said that the captain had been in touch.

"He said the ship has had quite a bit of work done but they are waiting for some parts to arrive from Germany, so we will have a few more weeks here. That's not a problem is it?"

"No," said Mia. "Not for me anyway. How about you. Are you happy to stay here.?"

"Yes, I can help dad with some paperwork. I know he sometimes stresses over things and if I can make life easier for him then all well and good."

Kevin and Richard spent hours in his study going through paperwork and putting things in order. Richard made a graph on the computer so that Kevin could see at a glance what bills needed paying and who owed him money. After they had called it a day Richard said he and Mia were able to stay for a few more weeks until the parts had arrived from Germany.

"Well that is good news. Now let's go and have a drink I think we deserve it."

Kevin and Sonya were walking around the garden when they stopped at the rose bush they had planted when Mia was born.

"Look," said Sonya, "the buds are coming out on the rose bush. We are going to get loads of flowers this year."

Kevin said he had Mr Hebden give it plenty of manure last year.

"Thank you, darling, we need to give this tree special attention as we do with the other plants we planted when the girls were born. As for that apple tree we planted when Graham was born do you remember when he tried to build a tree house in it and we lost most of its branches?

"Well it survived. Let's hope Kai does not want to build a tree house, if he does then he will have to do it in another tree," said Kevin.

Richard and Mia had to get back to the ship it was all fixed and ready to get back to sea. As they were saying their goodbyes, Kai ran to them and gave them both a picture he had drawn.

"This is for you to put up in your cabins so that you can remember us all."

Mia said. "We will never forget you but looking at your lovely picture every day will be the best thing."

As they got into the car, Mr Parr started the engine and the whole family waved from the steps. Mia had tears in her eyes but she tried to hide them from Richard but he had seen them.

"Never mind lass, we will see them soon."

Arriving at the station Mr Parr got their luggage out. "Take care both of you."

"Thank you," said Richard and they both headed to the train which was about to leave.

Sitting at the window, Mia looked out towards the front of the train while Richard went and got them both a coffee.

Seating himself beside her, Richard gave her the coffee and said. "Are you okay now?"

"Yes, thank you. I don't like saying goodbye, but then not many people do."

When they arrived at the ship Richard reported to the captain while Mia went to the galley to see what was needed. Looking around, she noticed that some of the food was very low, so she went to see the head chef who told her that they were expecting a delivery soon.

"Let's hope it arrives before we set sail."

"Oh, it will. We are not expected to leave until the day after tomorrow."

When the delivery arrived, Mia tried to get the tins onto the shelves in the larder when she noticed that some of the tins were from France. *How strange* she thought. She counted how many had French labels on them. She went to look for Richard and found him walking towards the galley.

"Can I ask you something?"

"Yes, do you have a problem?"

"Well, we have just had a delivery and as I was putting the tins in the larder, I noticed that some of them were from France. We have about fifty tins and I don't know what is in them."

Richard was intrigued and asked her to show him. On seeing the tins, he took one and started to open it on the work surface. As he could speak French, he saw that the label did not mention any food. When he had taken the lid off, he saw that it had a large bag inside that was wrapped in plastic and taped up.

"Well, I think we have found a stash of drugs. I had better get the captain down here."

Richard got onto the radio while he and Mia stayed in the galley to stop anyone trying to get to the tins. When the captain arrived, he had a look and then called the police to come and investigate who had ordered them, and where they had come from. Thus, the ship could not sail the next day as the police had to interview every crew member on board and look through all the paperwork to see who had ordered the food. It took them weeks; and after finding out who had placed the order and tracing the delivery company, the police found three men who were responsible for the drugs. Two worked for the delivery company and one was a crew member who worked on the ship as an engineer. He was court-martialled and put into prison for many years.

Paulette was busy at work when she saw on the notice board that some new posts were coming up and one she really took a liking to. It was a teaching post at the hospital. Writing down the details, she decided to download the form before leaving work that evening. Having sent the form off, she was glad that she had done it fast, as she was sure the job would be very popular with the other nurses.

After a month, she was invited to an interview for the post. Entering the interview room, she sat waiting with the other nurses. One by one they were called. The chairperson was an oldish man who Paulette thought must have been a doctor in his time. He sat at the head of the table with two matrons at each side of him; and beside them were two nurses. They all asked her loads of questions which she thought she had answered very well.

Eventually, they said. "Thank you for coming; we will let you know as soon as possible one way or another, if you have got the job."

Standing up, Paulette went to each of them and shook their hands. "Thank you."

Linda was hard at work booking holidays for her customers when one of her colleagues asked where she was going for her honeymoon.

"I don't know, we haven't decided where yet, but I do fancy either somewhere hot, small and private or a castle in Scotland."

Her colleagues laughed. "You do have quite a romantic mind. I am sure you will get the honeymoon you want."

Phillip was on his way to South Africa. His flight left in the early hours. He would be away for two weeks, and then he was flying home with a new plane and crew. Arriving at the airport in South Africa, he was doing his normal checks before leaving the plane. The crew were very nice and knew the routine. First, they would check to make sure that every customer had their belongings. Then they would walk up and down the plane to see if anything had been left behind. Then they would let the cleaners onto the plane and then go to their hotels. After a few days off relaxing and looking around South Africa they had to return to England.

Getting onto the new plane was just what Phillip looked forward to. It was a spanking new plane and a double decker at that. The cabin crew had doubled in size so Phillip had to introduce himself and his co-pilot, and then they did the normal checks before starting the engines. This took longer than usual as they had to make sure what all the switches were for, while the rest of the crew got the passengers seated, ready for take-off. The flight home was smooth and they managed to gain some time; so, after landing in London twenty minutes early and then showing staff the new plane, Phillip was eager to get home to Linda.

He was about to go on leave for three weeks; but before he could get out of the building there was a surprise party for him in the staff lounge. Balloons, gifts and cards were on the table with a few bottles of wine and champagne.

Everyone shouted, "Cheers!" as he walked into the room.

Phillip was almost in tears. He had not expected a party. He just wanted to have a quiet drink and then slip away and get married.

Upon arriving at his future in-laws' home, Linda came to the door to meet him. He said the crew had organised a party for him and his car was full of gifts, cards and balloons. After emptying the car, Phillip and Linda sat in the lounge chatting and then the topic turned to the honeymoon.

"Where have you decided to take me on our honeymoon?" Linda asked.

"You will just have to wait and see, but I suggest you pack some warm clothes."

Linda had been hoping that they would be going to Scotland. There were plenty of castles there and some lovely walks.

Chapter Nine

Linda and Phillip's wedding went without a hitch, Sonya and Kevin were so proud of their daughter. She had worked hard all her life and had now found the man of her dreams. Paulette and Mia were bridesmaids. Graham was best man and little Kai was a pageboy. After the reception the happy couple were off on their honeymoon. Linda still had no idea where they were going, so after saying goodbye to everyone they got into the sports car that was waiting outside the hotel with ribbons and old cans tied to the back.

They were alone at last, driving along country roads. After driving for what seemed hours Phillip pulled into a long driveway; and right there in front of them was a mansion. At first Linda thought it was a hotel, but Phillip said no it was a property that belonged to the family. They only used it for six months of the year. Linda asked where the family went for the other six months of the year.

"Well, they go to either France, America or Australia. They are in fact off to Australia next weekend."

"Why did you never mention this before?"

Phillip turned to face Linda. "My family do not have titles like yours. We are hardworking and grounded. We do not have servants. If you want a drink, you get up and get it yourself."

Linda was shocked to hear Phillip talking like this. Strange things were going around in her head. *Had she given him the impression that she wanted servants to wait on her hand and foot once they were married? No she had not and the staff who worked for her parents had been with them for years. Her parents had treated them with respect and as part of the family. They would have to have a talk about this later when they were not on honeymoon.*

After a couple of days at her new family's home, they headed off further north; this time towards Scotland. The castle they arrived at was on top of a steep hill. Part of it was a ruin but it had had a lot of work done to it over the years. The inside was out of this world! The rooms were decorated with velvet wallpaper and red carpets with large rugs all over the place. In each room, the fireplaces were so big you could stand up in them and the kitchen was part old fashioned and part modern. There was everything you could possibly need. Linda asked how many people were staying there.

Phillip said. "Just us."

He said he was going to unpack and then go for a walk and when he got back he wanted his meal on the table. That made Linda very angry; so, after watching him leave, she went down to the kitchen, put raw food out on a tray, carried it up to the dining room, placed the tray on the table with a knife and fork wrapped in a napkin, and then got a large plate and placed it at the head of the table with a couple of glasses one for wine and the other for water.

When Phillip arrived back, he called out for Linda, and when he didn't get a reply, he went looking for her. He found her in the dining room sitting near the fire, and then he turned to look at the table, expecting to see his meal ready but what he did see was a tray full of fresh vegetables.

"What is this?" He said.

"Well you never said you wanted it cooked."

Linda could see his face going red, but she stood her ground. After a while he calmed down and apologised for being such a bastard.

Linda said. "We have only just got married and if you think I am going to be at your beck and call, you are going to be disappointed. We are equal and there is no way I am going to be a skivvy for you."

After that, Phillip became very tentative towards Linda and the honeymoon started again. The rest of the time in Scotland was pleasant enough although it was very cold; and the only way they could get warm in the castle was to have a glass of whisky at night, sitting in front of the fire.

Driving home, the weather turned from rain to snow. The driving was hard for the small sports car. It was skidding all over the road; so halfway home, they decided to stop for the night at the first hotel or pub they came across. The big sign said – *Royal Oak Pub, rooms available,* so, pulling up in the carpark, they walked into the pub and asked the landlord if he had a room available.

"Yes," came the answer from behind the bar.

There, standing at the end of the bar was a lovely lady who looked like a film star with long red hair that flowed over her shoulders. She was dressed in a green velvety dress. Linda was mesmerised by her beauty.

"Come this way and I will get you your key and show you to your room."

"Thank you," said Phillip.

"The room is perfect. Are we able to have a meal this evening or is the kitchen closed for the night."

"I shall leave a menu at the bar for you, and when you are ready let me know, and I shall tell the chef. We serve the last meal at ten, so you have plenty of time."

The meal was hot and filling – just what Linda wanted. They sat at the bar until it was closing time then they went up to their room.

Early in the morning, Linda started to itch. Her legs were being bitten by fleas. Getting out of bed and turning on the light, she looked down at her legs. There were big red spots all over her legs and arms.

"That's all I need," she said.

Phillip got out of bed to see what was wrong. He looked at Linda and said. "Should I get the owners?"

"No. We will deal with them in the morning, but I am not sleeping in that bed."

Phillip looked at his arms and legs. There were only a few spots so he slept on top of the covers with his coat over himself while Linda slept on the sofa.

In the morning, they went downstairs to tell the owners that the bed had fleas and they had both been almost eaten alive. The couple who ran the place were very apologetic and said there would be no charge for the accommodation, and wished them all the best in their married life.

Driving home, the roads were clear and they managed to get home in good time. Luckily, Paulette was home so after she had a look at Linda's legs and arms, she gave them some cream to rub on their bodies after they had had a shower. Coming downstairs after her shower, Linda was talking to her mother and sister in the lounge, while Phillip was talking to Kevin in his study about the castle.

Kevin said. "It sounds like you both had a great time in Scotland."

"Oh we did, but it was very cold."

Linda told her mother and sister a different story. "The castle was lovely but when we got there Phillip unpacked his bags and then went for a walk on his own and demanded that I had to have his meal ready for him when he got back."

Sonya's eyes almost popped out of her head. "He said what?"

Linda then told them that she went to the kitchen, got a tray full of raw vegetables, placed them on the dining table and set the table for him at the top of the table with a glass for the wine and one for water.

"It turned out that he thought that I wanted servants. He said that his family don't have any servants. And that they spend six months of the year abroad either in France, America or Australia."

"Did you put him right on that one?" Paulette asked.

"I sure did. I told him that I had no idea he was thinking in that way and that if I had wanted servants, I would have mentioned it. Anyway, after that was sorted we had a good time in Scotland."

All the wedding gifts were in one of the bedrooms for them to sort out and take to their new home.

Looking at them all; Linda said. "We had better make a list of who gave us what."

After opening the first one, which was from Graham, Sally and Kai, Linda was almost in tears. It was the most beautiful bed linen with their initials embroidered on it. The rest of the gifts were opened and the list was very long. After they had some lunch, the gifts were then put into a car and taken to their new home which was about three miles away.

Carrying Linda over the threshold, Phillip put her down in the front hall, gave her a big kiss. "Welcome home darling, let me show you the house. This is the lounge and dining room. The kitchen is through here. We have a pantry and a laundry room. Upstairs, we have four bedrooms. Our room has a en-suite bathroom and there is a family bathroom. Outside, we have a garden with fruit trees and part of the lawn can be turned into a vegetable plot. There is a single garage with room to put your car and maybe some shelves against that wall. What do you think? Do you like it? I think we will be very happy here. Shall we go and have a drink, and then we can start emptying the car I know you are keen to start organising your kitchen."

Linda made coffee while Phillip started to unpack the car. The kitchen items were placed on the counter, so Linda could start thinking where it would be best to put them. She changed her mind loads of times before she decided on the best places. After unpacking everything, she then went upstairs to their room and made the bed with the beautiful bed linen. Standing back and looking at it, she started to cry; it was so perfect. Then she heard Phillip coming upstairs; so, wiping the tears away she looked out of the window and said. "I think the vegetable patch should go that side of the garden where the sun will be first thing in the morning."

"Yes, I agree. We can plan that some other time, but first I think we had better get some shopping done or we won't have any food to eat this evening." With that Linda got her coat on and found some shopping bags.

Linda looked at Phillip and said. "This is going to be very strange for both of us having to do the weekly shop."

"Yes but we will soon get used to it."

Phillip was due to fly to America in a couple of weeks and Linda was due back at work at the travel agents. She had missed her staff but going back to work was days away, so she was determined to make the most of the time she had with Phillip. She asked him how long he would be away this time. He said about ten days unless they want him to fly anywhere else. He would phone her if he was going to be away longer. That's good.

She said. "I think I will look into painting one of the bedrooms. I could do with a sunny sewing room or even a craft room."

Phillip asked her. "What sort of crafts do you do?"

"Oh, I can turn my hand to anything, but I can do my knitting downstairs."

While Phillip was away, Linda invited her sister and mother round for coffee. They sat in the garden as it was a lovely hot day. Sonya wanted to know what they planned for the vegetable plot.

"We are thinking of having about four raised beds. We can grow lots of fresh veg. We have some fruit trees but we are not sure what type."

Sonya said. "I can send Mr Hebden round. He can give you some advice on what is best for you and give the trees a trim."

"Thank you Mum, that would be great."

Driving home, Paulette and Sonya were talking about the home Linda and Phillip had bought.

"It's a grand house but don't you think it's a bit large for them?"

Sonya replied. "That is just what I was thinking but maybe they got it cheap. Anyway, I am sure Linda will turn it into a lovely home."

Pulling up into the driveway, Sonya and Paulette got out of the car and went inside the house to see Graham and Kai who were in the lounge with Kevin.

"Hello you two, where have you been?"

"Oh, we went to see Linda and the new house it's very grand."

"Oh, before we forget, can Mr Hebden go and see Linda. She wants some advice on the garden and some of the trees will need a trim soon."

"Yes, I will see if he is free this week."

Kai was playing with his toys on the rug. He liked to turn his building blocks into fences so he could make his toy horse's jump over them. Paulette said she thought he would be a show jumper when he grew up.

"No Aunty, I want to be a pilot just like my Daddy." This made Graham smile.

Kevin and Sonya had a big anniversary coming up. They had been married for almost fifty years. They both wanted a big party, but the problem was where and when to have it. They would see if Mia and Richard could get some time away from the ship. Then there was Phillip and Linda. The rest of the family were easy. Kevin said if they could not find a place to cater for everyone then how about getting a large marquee in the garden?

"We could get a catering company to do the food."

"That's an idea but let's think about it," replied Sonya. "We have plenty of time. Our anniversary is not until the summer."

"Okay," said Kevin.

Christine wanted to see her father, so she sent him a letter. When it arrived at the house it was put on Kevin's desk with the other post. He did not open it straight away but put it aside to open when he had more time to read it without being disturbed. Later that evening, he went into his study and opened the letter. Sitting back in his chair, he started to read. Christine was getting married and wanted her father to give her away. Her fiancé was Paul Jackson who was a police officer. Kevin read the rest of the letter, but kept going back to the part where she said she was getting married. *I cannot believe she is getting married she is far too young and who is this Paul Jackson.*

After a while, Kevin went to see Sonya and told her the news.

"Do you think she wants you to pay for the wedding?"

"No, I don't think so; well, she never mentioned it. I truly think she is far too young to get married." "Well, the other thing is she might have got herself pregnant and this Paul Jackson is pushing her to marry him before the baby arrives," said Sonya.

Kevin hoped that was not the reason for the wedding. "It looks like I shall have to write her a letter, asking Christine to come and introduce her fiancé Paul."

Sonya thought it was a good idea, but said. "Write it tomorrow after you have had time to think things through."

Sitting in his study, reading through the letter again, Kevin started to write to his daughter. He started by offering congratulations; then he asked if he could meet Paul. He suggested that they could meet somewhere local. 'It would be best if you don't come to the family home. Let me know what you and Paul think, Love Dad'.

A few days later, another letter arrived from Christine. It arrived at the house when Kevin was out for the day. On his return he went to his study to open the letter. It read. 'Dad, if you are free this Sunday we can meet you at the coffee shop on the main street at about eleven. We cannot stay long as Paul is on an afternoon shift. I hope you are well, see you soon Christine.'

Kevin wrote straight back to say that was fine; and that he would be on his own as he did not want to involve Sonya at that point. 'She knows you are getting married and wishes you both well. See you on Sunday, love Dad.'

On Sunday at eleven, Kevin was sitting in the coffee shop waiting for Christine and Paul to arrive. He glanced out of the window, watching a mother with her two little boys. He thought that they must be on their way to the playground as they had their wellingtons and winter coats on. Just then the coffee shop door opened and Christine and Paul walked in. Kevin stood up and kissed Christine on the cheek and then shook Paul's hand. The café owner came to take their orders; and then Kevin asked some questions about Paul and why they were in such a rush for the wedding.

Christine said. "It's because we love each other and, no, I am not pregnant."

Paul was tall with dark hair; a well-built man. He had been with the police for four years. He had his own home and his parents lived close by. He had two sisters and one brother. After talking a while Kevin realised that Christine had not told Paul anything about her mother as this could have jeopardised his work with the police force. She had not told him her father was a lord which Kevin was pleased about. Kevin then asked when and where the wedding would be. They said it would be at the registry office in three weeks' time at twelve noon; then after that, guests would go to the Golden Fleece pub. Christine asked her dad if he would walk her down the aisle.

"Yes, I would be proud to walk you down the aisle," he answered. "Is it going to be a quiet do?"

"Yes, just family and a couple of friends. My brother is my best man and Christine's brother Andrew is going to take the wedding photos."

Kevin was not sure if Andrew would keep quiet about his father being a lord, but if it came out at the wedding, things could turn out to be difficult for Paul. Then Kevin realised that the wedding photos would be in the newspaper and everyone would know it was Lord Swan who was giving his daughter away. Kevin thought about it for a moment and decided to tell Paul that he was a lord. If he said it did not matter then he would leave it and not bring up the topic again. After Kevin had told him the news, Paul did not know what to say. He thought about it and said that he had no problem with being a titled gent. As long as it did not stop him from marrying Christine then nothing else mattered.

Later, while Paul was at work he asked one of his colleagues to see if there was anything he could find on a Lord Swan. His colleague was inquisitive and asked why he had asked.

"Oh, he is my future father-in-law. I have just met him and he seems to be a well-bred gent but I have this feeling he is not telling me something."

"You were right; this Lord Swan had an affair with a woman called Shirley and they had two children Christine and Andrew. Shirley whipped one of Lord Swans children and ended up in prison for child abuse. She was let out and put into a safe house and then she got close to one of Lord Swans children and broke her nose. Now, she is back in prison and is not due for release for another seven years."

Having heard that news, Paul had to go and see his boss just to make sure the news would not have any consequences on him being a police officer.

His boss said. "Thank you for bringing this to my attention. I shall have to report it to the head of the police and I'll get back to you as soon as possible."

Kevin arrived home to find a letter on his desk. It was from the prison. He opened it and read the short note. Shirley had asked for a day release so she could attend the wedding of her daughter.

Kevin sat in his chair and said to himself. "There is no way would she be coming to the wedding."

He did not know if he should mention it to Christine and the rest of the family. *As things could turn very nasty,* he thought. What if she caused a scene. Also she would be handcuffed to a prison officer all the time which would attract attention. That was it. She would not be coming to the wedding. He was determined not to say anything at all; so replying to the letter, he said no she was not invited and under no circumstances was she to contact him or his family again.

Chapter Ten

Paul and Christine's wedding went off without a hitch. Kevin walked with her down to the room where everyone waited. As soon as they entered the room, the registrar asked everyone to stand. Then, turning to his wife Sonya, he sat down beside her and the ceremony went ahead. His mind was wandering when Sonya nudged him in the ribs as the registrar asked if the father of the bride would like to go into the back room and sign the register with Christine and Paul and his parents. Then, they all went to the Golden Fleece pub for the reception. The drinks started to flow and the photographer started taking photos of the guests. Then everyone was asked to take their places at the tables.

Looking around Kevin and Sonya could not find their place names.

They were still walking around the room when Paul said. "Kevin, Sonya you are both at the top table with us."

Sonya felt a bit embarrassed when some of the guests looked at them both. Seated next to his daughter, Kevin asked Sonya if he had to write a speech.

"I don't think so; anyway it's too late now."

When it came to the speeches, Kevin had to wing it. He was used to speaking at dinners, so he made a short father's speech and then sat down and then the father of the groom gave a short speech. After the meal, the dancing started while the staff cleared the tables. It was getting late and Sonya thought it was time they left. All the older guests had gone either to their rooms or home and left the younger ones to dance the night away.

Kevin said goodbye to his daughter and wished them both a long and happy married life. Paul gave Sonya a kiss on the cheek and thanked them both for coming.

He said. "I know Christine was happy that you both came and when we get back from our honeymoon we will be in touch."

Driving home Kevin and Sonya were chatting in the back of the car about Paul's parents. "They seemed nice enough, but some of the guests gave us the evil eye when Paul said we were at the top table."

"You get that from time to time; especially when guests are jealous. Some people say who do they think they are? Just as you pass them, knowing you will hear them. It makes me so angry as there is no need for it."

Arriving home, Kevin walked into the lounge to find a fire burning and two glasses and a bottle of wine on the table, waiting for them with a small card.

After reading it, he said to Sonya. "That is nice! Here; it's from Paul and Christine thanking us for sharing their special day." They relaxed by the fire drank some of the wine and then went up to their room.

The next day Mr Parr was washing the car when he found a gold ring on the driveway. It was a lady's ring, a very small one at that, and he had no idea who it belonged to, so he went inside and gave it to Sonya who had no idea who it belonged to. She put it on the desk in Kevin's office with a note saying that it had been found by Mr Parr on the driveway. When Kevin came home after visiting Paulette, he saw the note and put the ring in a locked drawer. It was lunchtime and Mrs Richardson had made some sausage rolls and fresh bread. The aroma in the house was making him hungry.

After lunch, Kevin and Sonya went to see Sally and Graham. Kai was at school and would soon arrive at home, so Graham and Sonya went to collect him. He had no idea his nana was collecting him. He produced a big smile when he saw her. Her arms were held out to give him a big hug and kiss.

"You have grown," said Sonya.

"That's because he is always eating," said Graham. "He is having a growing spurt. I think he is going to be taller than me when he gets older."

Walking home Kai held his nana's hand, while telling her all about his day at school and his friends. Billy was his best friend. He had ginger hair and freckles on his face.

"That's nice," said Sonya. "Is he your age?"

"Yes, and his mother is in the RAF like Daddy, but they don't work together."

"Well, there are a lot of people working in the air force. They all have special talents. That is why they do different jobs."

When they arrived home, Kai went to find his mum. He wanted something to eat, but she was busy in the kitchen preparing tea.

"You can have a small snack as tea will not be long."

He was reaching into the cookie jar when he noticed a small field mouse sitting on the window sill; looking at him through the window. Kai did not move or make a sound. He was mesmerised by the little creature. His mum watched him and wondered what was happening. Then, she followed his gaze and saw the field mouse sitting on the window sill. Her first thought was to shoo the mouse away but then she changed her mind.

"Hello little mouse."

Kai turned to look at his mum and said. "Can I keep him Mum?"

"No darling, he is a wild animal and he has a family of his own to look after, but I am sure we will see him again."

The mouse ran away down the garden and across the field. Kai looked out each day to see if he could see the mouse, but he never came.

Kai was thinking about the mouse, and thought he would draw a picture and write a small story about the field mouse, which he named cheeky chops. It took him most of the day, but when he had finished he took it to show his mum. After reading the story and looking at the pictures he had drawn, Sally said it was a lovely story and the pictures were very good.

"I think we should show daddy when he gets home from work!"

So, putting the little book on the table, Kai waited for his daddy to come home. Half an hour later, in walks daddy. Kai ran to meet him at the door and said he had done a story about a mouse and had drawn some pictures.

"Come and read it Daddy. Mummy said it was very good."

"Let me take my coat and shoes off first son." Then, walking into the kitchen, he saw the story book on the table. Sitting on the chair, he started to read about the mouse called cheeky chops. After he finished reading, Graham looked at Sally and said. "I think we have a budding author in the family."

Sally nodded. They both thought it should be published; so, that evening Graham started to find someone who would be able to publish it, it was not an easy thing and took quite a few days to find someone who could help, in the end they got a phone call to say it was going to be published but they wanted Kai to have a photograph taken for the cover of the book, so without telling Kai, they took him to the photographer to have his photo taken then sent it to the publisher.

Within weeks, the book was on the shelves and there on the front cover was Kai smiling. The publisher had sent a box of books for Kai to give to his family and friends. When Kai got home from school he noticed the box with his name on it. His dad had said it had come for him and that he should open it.

Opening the box, he found his face on a book and then he read the title of the book. It read: my little cheeky chops. Looking up at his mum and dad. Kai could not think what to say, but then he said. "It's my story."

"Yes, darling. We both thought it was a lovely story and we wanted everyone to read it. It's in the shops so everyone can buy it and read about your little cheeky chops. We had it published and you have some money which we have put into your bank account for when you get older. You can say you are a published author now."

Kai kept one book for Mia for when she came home after her long duty on the ship. She was due home in a couple of weeks and everyone looked forward to seeing her. Kai counted the days when his father said. "It is only four days now and then Aunty Mia will be home."

Kai turned to his mother and said. "Can we make a cake for when she gets home? I know she likes a lemon cake."

"Yes darling, we can make it the day before." Kai started to rub his hands together in excitement and then went to his room and got one of his books to write a message in it.

It read: "To my Aunty Mia, I miss you when you are away on the ship and look forward to your leave. All my love, Kai."

Mia was at the station on her way home when she heard a car horn. Turning to see who it could be, she saw Mr Parr and Kai holding her bags. She held out her arms as she saw Kai running towards her. "Hello my darling, this is a nice surprise. Where are your mummy and daddy."

"They are at home. They said I could come with Mr Parr to collect you."

"That is so nice come on then let's get my bags in the car. I need a cup of tea."

Arriving home, Kai went into the house and said to his mummy. "Aunty Mia is in need of a cup of tea. Is the kettle on?"

"It will be soon. Let's go and see Aunty Mia first." Mia had just walked into the lounge when Kai gave her the gift. He had wrapped it up in some lovely paper.

"What is this? It's not my birthday."

"Open it Aunty Mia." Kai was jumping up and down, eager for her to open it.

Looking up at her was Kai's face. Opening the book, she read the inscription on the first page. Mia had tears in her eyes.

"I wrote a book and had it published. This is your copy. I hope you like reading it."

Mia gave Kai a big hug and loads of kisses. "Thank you darling I am sure I will."

After catching up with Graham and Sally it was time to go home. Mr Parr waited at the car.

Mia said. "See you all tomorrow."

Getting into the car, Mia turned to wave and then she saw Kai. He was running after her. "You left your book on the table."

"Thank you darling. I shall start reading it tonight." Giving him a kiss and making sure that the car door was closed, she blew a kiss and then they were on the road to her parents' home.

Kevin and Sonya were in the lounge when they heard the front door open. They heard Mia's voice. She was calling out. "Is anyone at home?"

"Yes darling, we are in the lounge."

Sonya was sitting near the window knitting and Kevin was in his favourite chair, reading the newspaper. Kevin got up to kiss his daughter and then Mia went over to give her mother a kiss.

"How was your journey home? Did Mr Parr get to the station on time?"

"Yes, and to my surprise Kai was there as well. Don't worry I did ask him if his mum and dad knew he was with Mr Parr, so we dropped him at home and he gave me a signed book he had written and had published."

"What? Kai has written a book and had it published."

"Yes, here it is."

Passing the book over to her mother, Mia said she had told Kai she would read it that night. Sonya passed the book to Kevin.

Looking at the cover, he said. "I like the photo in the front." Then he opened it and read the inscription. "That is amazing! We now have an author in the family. What I don't understand is why he never mentioned it to us."

"I am sure he will tell you, and he may even give you a copy of the book."

Mia went up to her room and got changed before dinner. Hanging up her uniform and putting all her things on her dresser and the rest of her clothes in the chest of drawers, she headed downstairs to where her father had poured drinks.

"Well; tell us how things are on the ship. Are you in charge of the galley yet?"

"No, but I do have some new trainee staff. They are a good bunch and eager to learn; but time will tell if they can handle the rough seas. It took me almost two months before I found my sea legs."

A letter came from the prison to say that Shirley was up for parole. She was due to appear in front of a judge within the next two weeks and if any of the family wanted to attend the hearing they could but it would have to be requested in writing. Mia said she would like to go but her mother did not want to attend. Kevin said he would write a letter stating that he and Mia would be there.

"Are you sure about this?" Sonya asked. "You know you don't have to go."

"I know Mum, but if I can change the ruling then it will be good won't it."

"I suppose so, but don't get your hopes up."

Kevin wrote the letter, and it was sent first class mail.

The next morning he asked Mr Parr to get the car ready as he was taking Sonya and Mia out for the day and he had booked a table at the riverside restaurant. The restaurant was normally booked up for two months in advance; but Lord and Lady Swan always got a table when they phoned in advance. The shopping trip was just what Sonya and Mia needed. They went into most of the shops and handed the bags to Kevin to hold, and then went into the next shop. Mia looked at her dad. He was laden with bags and was not looking happy, so she said to her mum that they should call it a day.

"I think dad has had enough."

"Okay darling. We have spent loads anyway." Turning to Kevin, Sonya said. "What time is the table booked for, as we are getting a little peckish."

"It's booked for two p.m. so we can leave now and get there about two-ish."

"That sounds good," said Mia. "My stomach is rumbling a little."

The restaurant had a table ready for them when they arrived. It was in a quiet corner and one of the staff had put up a decorative partition, so they had privacy. The meal itself was delicious; all washed down with a couple of bottles of fine wine. After they had finished, they headed back to the car where Mr Parr waited. Driving home, Mia asked her dad if everything was okay as he seemed to be worried about something.

"I am okay darling. Nothing for you to worry about."

"But I am worried about you. Now come on! Tell me what is the matter? Are you ill? or has something happened that you don't want me to know about?"

Kevin replied. "It's just that if Shirley were to be released from prison she may come to the house even more than before."

"Let's not get ahead of ourselves," said Sonya. "I am sure the court will put restrictions on her movements."

Mia wondered if she should go to court in her uniform or not. She asked her parents what she should wear to court, and they both said something smart.

"You may be photographed when you come out."

She said. "Should I wear my uniform?"

"I would wear a smart dress," said Sonya. "This has nothing to do with the navy it would tell Shirley that you will be away from home for months at a time."

"You always give good advice Mum; thank you."

Shirley's day in court was here. She was handcuffed to a prison officer and taken to the seat behind a Perspex sheet. Looking around the court, she noticed Kevin and Mia, She waved to them but they ignored her. Her solicitor told her to stay calm and to listen to the judge.

"Ignore everyone here and don't make eye contact with anyone you might know."

Of course he meant Kevin and Mia.

As the judge came into the court, the usher said. "All rise."

The judge said. "Be seated, this court is now in session. We are to discover whether the prisoner Shirley has reformed enough to be released. If there is anything at all that worries you, then please speak now."

The solicitors went up to the judge to discuss matters; then after about three minutes had passed, they both went to their seats. The opening statements were read out. The first one was from Kevin. He had written a letter saying that Shirley had put his family through enough; and that if she were to be released, he asked the court if she could be placed far away from him and his family; and that if she ever came within a short distance from his home, then she would be arrested. The judge agreed, and then the other solicitor got to his feet and said that Shirley had agreed with that and that she had been a model inmate; she had reformed herself and had worked hard to keep her temper under control.

Shirley's solicitor agreed. "We don't think Shirley is a threat to anyone; so I plead to your honour that Shirley is ready to be let out into the world."

The judge said. "I am sure we can come to some agreement on where to place Shirley – far away from the children she hurt all those years ago."

The judge said he would deliver his verdict later on in the day, and then he stood up and left the courtroom.

Chapter Eleven

Graham, Sally and the baby girl came home from hospital, they had arrived at the family home to collect Kai, everyone was there and they wanted to know her name, well said Graham that is up to Kai. After thinking for a while Kai went over to his mum who was cuddling his sister, looking at her he said " Hello Grace I am your big brother Kai". Grace gave a big smile then went fast asleep.

As the years rolled on the Swan family were getting on with life, Kevin and Sonya were happy babysitting and going on holiday. Linda and Phillip were doing their thing; visiting friends abroad. Graham and Sally were enjoying being parents to two wonderful children. Paulette was still nursing and single. Richard was the Admiral of the *Royal Outlander* and was on the lookout for a lady to share his life with. As for Mia, she was head chef of the *Royal Outlander*; working hard and enjoying life at sea.

Kai left school and joined the RAF. He flies big jets now, just like his dad did; and Grace grew up to be a doctor just like her mum.

The End

The author

Sue Armstrong was born in Newark in the UK.
Her family moved around so much that she is
not aware of which exams she passed if any. She
worked as a shop assistant, a childminder and an
auxiliary nurse. Sue likes to knit, cook, write, read
books, loves playing card and board games. Life
was hard for Sue. Don't Lie to Me Young Lady is
her first book based on her life experiences. She
is retired and a widow. She has two sons, both of
whom are married.